Aritha van Herk was born in 1954 in central Alberta. She grew up on a farm near the village of Edberg, just a few miles from the Battle River, an area that she still writes about. She published her first poem when she was twelve, and her first published story won the Miss Chatelaine Short Fiction Award in 1976. In 1978 she won the Seal First Novel Award for *Judith*, and in 1981 she published her second novel, *The Tent Peg*. Her third novel, *No Fixed Address*, appeared in 1986, the same year in which she was selected as one of the ten best fiction writers in Canada under forty-five years of age.

Her work has been published in eleven countries and nine languages, and she has traveled extensively, giving lectures and readings from her work. She has also co-edited two anthologies of fiction, *More Stories from Western Canada* and *West of Fiction*.

Ms. van Herk received her M.A. in English from the University of Alberta in 1978. She is currently Associate Professor of English and Creative Writing at the University of Calgary. She is married to Robert Sharp, who is an exploration geologist.

Aritha van Herk

The Tent Peg

New Canadian Library N196

McClelland and Stewart

The Canadian Publishers
McClelland and Stewart
481 University Avenue
Toronto, Ontario
M5G 2E9

Canadian Cataloguing in Publication Data

Van Herk, Aritha, 1954-
   The tent peg

ISBN 0-7710-9390-X

I. Title

PS8593.A53T46   C813´.54   C81-094096-5
PR9199.3.V35T46

Printed and bound in Canada by Webcom Ltd.

For Sharon Batt, Sharon Smith, Mary Sainsbury, Leah Flater, and all my women friends who carry tent pegs of their own.

For Ian and Sue, Alex and Linda, Dave and Ginny, Doug and Barb, June and Reg, who told me stories.

And once again for Bob, who always helps.

J.L.

Under the pale outrage of a breaking sky, the plane thuds. As if the ground flings the reverberation of our passing back at us from the cracked and wrinkled face of the tundra, expressionless white but for a few black lines of water.

Beside the pilot, Mackenzie traces our flight, finger on the map. The shapes of the lakes below are an impelled deception; if you raise your eyes for one moment, you become instantly lost.

The pilot whistles at his controls. "I just fly," he said when Mackenzie asked him about the breakup. "I just fly."

Their voices in front of me ebb; beneath the plane the land wheels in an unending hesitation of sameness. And yet, it is ever-changing, white snow and black water a striated spectrum. I am mesmerized, frozen here looking down. Two hours we have flown transfixed by that fatal design. For it is dangerous. Skull teeth gleam through an invitation; the tundra can both restore and maim. No man lives to presume its power.

And then Mackenzie leans forward, pointing. "There," he says. "There. Can you land?"

The pilot banks, drops the plane, we seem to accelerate until we cruise just above the surface of the viscous ice, we are edging down, then abruptly he pulls the nose up.

"Nope."

"Come on," says Mackenzie urgently. "We've got to land."

"Can't," says the pilot. The plane climbs, nose pulled tight against the sky.

"Christ! I pay you to fly us all the way up here and you damn well won't even land!"

"Ice ain't safe. Candling."

"It'll hold an elephant."

The pilot sucks his teeth. "Nope."

"Come on, you've landed on soft ice before."

"I don't like it." He squints at Mackenzie. "You want to haul a Cessna up from the bottom of a lake?"

Mackenzie grunts. "Let's just look at it once more."

The wing dips and again we skim over the ice, seemingly perfect, only the telltale marks of black cracks spider the outer edge of the lake.

"Your neck," mutters the pilot.

"Don't do it if it's not safe, for Chrissake!"

"Hunnhh."

He pulls back the throttle control and then there is that bump and slide of the skis, a swish of wind that you do not feel or hear in the air, until the plane comes to a tentative stop at the far end of the lake.

When I dare to edge my way onto the creaking ice, Mackenzie is already on shore, digging in the snow. After a moment he straightens and squints up at the sun and then at me watching him and then at the pilot still sitting inside the plane.

I stand beside the wing, feel in the sky and the land and the ice a coating of silence, thick and gelid. There is no sound here, no sight, no smell, nothing. Numb, I stamp, to feel the ice shudder imperceptibly under my booted foot.

Above me, the pilot sticks his head out of the open door. "Come on!" he hollers.

Mackenzie kneels, kneads the ground again. Finally he nods and rises, rubbing his palms on the front of his jeans.

He takes a bound across that thin ribbon of water at the edge of the lake, seems to be standing solidly, when *crack!* His arms flail and one leg buckles through the ice. I run, but before I have gone five yards he crawls onto the splintered shelf and is up and heading for the plane, one blue-jeaned leg rivuleting water.

"Get in," he yells at me, and even before I have my door shut the pilot is roaring down the length of the lake again.

In the air, Mackenzie unbuckles and takes off his jeans,

rubs his leg dry with a rag the pilot fishes from under the seat.

"Look," he says to me without turning his head. "Sun-dogs."

I've never seen them before. I crane my neck at their triple-diamond deception. Which one is the sun? Impossible to tell.

The plane settles into a steady drone and now the sundogs chase us across the receding grayness below. The pilot eases back, seems to loosen his grip now that we are on our way home.

"What are you guys looking for?"

"Uranium," says Mackenzie absently, finger on the map spread across his bare knees.

The pilot whistles. "Unpopular."

Mackenzie only lifts one eyebrow. "Wait until the lights go out."

In Yellowknife he jumps off at the dock, carrying his wet jeans. We climb into our rented truck and drive to the hotel and I follow his green jockey shorts through the startled faces in the lobby and up the stairs to the room, thinking of that silence I heard out on the barrenlands, hovering and listening.

Mackenzie

I'm sitting in my hotel room, as close to the window as possible so I can get some light to fall across these maps. Nothing but tundra and lakes, lakes and tundra. Once you're out there, in amongst the moss and the occasional outcrop, you melt right down into the barrens. Not a dot of anyone anywhere. And I like it that way. Maybe why I come back up here every year, forty-one and still sleeping in a tent, still drinking the hair of the dog, still walking with the sun in my eyes. I should be in management, shirt and tie, shave my beard off, jog at lunch to keep the pot away. But Janice always took the kids to the coast for the summer and even now, I can't seem to break the habit. Everyone expects ol' Mackenzie to head for the bush in the middle of May; if I said I wanted a change, they'd be upset. And once you get out here nothing matters.

There's a knock on the door. "Door's open," I say and then realize that it must be the cook, due to arrive on the twelve-ten plane from Edmonton.

He stands there in the doorway, bent under the weight of his pack, a small, diffident boy wearing an old fedora hat. "Earl Mackenzie? I'm J.L. Supposed to be your cook."

He's younger and softer than I expected, but hell, I've had kids who were practically gourmets. Can't tell nothing until you taste their cooking.

I push back my chair. "Come on in."

He looks around hesitantly, then drops his pack in the corner. Good. He's smart enough to come with nothing more than a backpack. Had a cook one summer who flew in with a goddamn steamer trunk. And what could we do but sling that mother from camp to camp the five times we moved. With him hopping up and down on the ground, yelling at the chopper pilot, "Don't tip it, don't tip it, my knives will get damaged!" Should've told the pilot to dump it in the lake. A flaming faggot, that's what he was.

This one looks young and scared, but resilient enough. He doesn't take off his hat but sits on the bed and swings one booted foot. Bites his fingernails, I can see.

"Guess you can share with me until the rest of the crew arrive," I say. "They don't usually come in until we're ready to head out. I figured you would want time to sort the supplies and utensils, and of course, you've got to buy the food."

He nods, quick.

"First time you've been a cook up here?"

"Yes."

His voice is low and scratchy, as if it's just changing. Maybe he's younger than I thought. "How old are you?" I ask.

"Twenty-four."

I shrug and go back to my map. Takes a long time for some kids to grow up — maybe this summer'll do it for him.

"We're lucky we got this program," I say. "Hell of a lot more work walking up and down mountains than walking in the barrenlands."

"I guess so."

"We're flying out to the location to check the breakup this afternoon. Want to come?"

"Gee, thanks," he says. "I'd like that."

And maybe he's never ridden in a light plane before, but he doesn't show it, swings into the rear seat and buckles up as if this is going to be some jet ride. I hope he has a strong stomach; it's rough when the pilot flies low, and a windy spring day like this can make it feel like the plane is playing hopscotch.

I navigate. The pilot is bitchy as hell; they don't like flying in breakup. Use skis and you'll need floats; use floats and you'll need skis. Who can tell? It's that kind of country, changes her mind the minute your back is turned. I like the fickleness; it keeps you guessing. One minute it's sunshine and the next it's snowing, and you're caught out there without a downfill or even a rag to keep the wet off, only a packful of rocks on your back, chafing your soaked shirt against your skin.

Me, I always carry my own rocks. Assistants slow you down, ask questions, or else want to go after their own bright idea. You have to baby them and threaten them and coach them and make sure they don't break a leg. I like it out there alone. Alone with nothing around but tundra and quiet, the two of them holding each other down against the sky and their own expanse. It's bad enough having to spend three solid months with the same people in the same tent, everyone grating everyone else, half of them with tundra fever before the summer's even begun.

And I'm the party chief. I'm responsible. I'm the one who's got to keep them going, keep them from killing each other, get them out of bed in the morning, stop the poker games at midnight, delegate who digs the shitter, send in a report that says, yes, we're doing something out here, and no, we haven't been playing chicken with the helicopter.

There's the lake. If I can't find another mine here, I'll never find it anywhere. It's like Meteor Ridge — I've got the same feeling. This area is almost untouched; no one thinks there's anything good here and nobody knows we're going to find it this summer. Just don't tell the crew where you're going or they'll blab it around some barroom table and the next day there'll be three floatplanes landing on the lake two miles downwind and you'll have a staking rush on your hands. I don't have to worry about the cook. He doesn't know where the hell we are anyway.

"There," I say to the pilot. "There. Can you land?"

He eases the Cessna down nervously and even before he swoops up again, I know the bastard won't risk it. But it was twenty below up here a couple of weeks ago and the ice can't be candling that badly so I taunt him a bit, these fellows don't like to think they're afraid of anything, they all want to be heroes. And he does it, he mutters and scowls but he does it, and I jump out and run to the shore, check the ground, can we work or do we have to sit in Yellowknife another week?

The snow is tacky under my hands and the moss beneath it is not dry but springy soft. I stand and look at the sun and at the crouched plane, then I feel the ground again, feel it warming itself. Better get back on that Cessna before it sinks right through the ice in front of my eyes. I take a running jump from shore but know even before the crunch and the shock I haven't made it, I've got one leg soaking up that numb water while my other knee is still hanging onto the sludgy edge. The cook starts to run toward me but I haul myself onto the crumbling ice shelf and go for that plane, my leg already a frozen toothpick.

"Get in!" I holler and climb up hell for leather. The pilot doesn't need to be told, he just starts throttling down the ice. And I don't think the cook even saw that double line of black water that the skis tracked behind. He just stares at me while I tear myself out of those wet jeans and try to rub some circulation back into my leg. Can't put my pants back on, so I wrap my coat around my waist and rub until the twinges tell me that my leg's still there. Too goddamn close for comfort.

That cook just doesn't react, he acts like this happens every day. Sits back there quiet as a mouse and watches that frozen country spreading herself under our shadow as if he's mesmerized, hooked already. Maybe he's scared. I don't mind that he's quiet, I hate the ones that won't stop talking. They're usually the guys who end up being afraid of the dark, what dark there is up here.

And he doesn't even rib me about walking around in my gaunch, meekly follows me through the lobby of the hotel with the tourists at the newsstand gawking and Gail in the candy shop grinning so that I know tomorrow it'll be all over town that Earl Mackenzie was walking around mother naked.

13

The people who run the hotel just nod and ignore me. I've been coming here for years and I've done stranger things.

But the kid has me puzzled, none of the strut and talk of most guys who come north. Keeps that old fedora on and stays quiet. Even after a few beers and a good steak, I catch him watching me with that guarded look on his face until finally I'm starting to wonder whether I've got a silent type on my hands — which isn't bad since they don't seem to mind the isolation — or if he's running away from something and this seemed like the best place to come. Makes me uneasy as hell. I don't like the kids who blurt out everything right away but it's easier to deal with them for the rest of the summer. No secrets.

And he does seem odd, something that I can't quite put my finger on in his silence, a reticence that is not shyness, but protection. Well, before the summer's over, I'll know him well enough. As long as he can cook, I don't give a damn whether he's got a tongue or not.

"What's J.L. stand for?" I ask, chewing my steak.

He looks at me blackly and says, "Nothing. Just J.L."

"You mean your initials don't stand for a name?"

He scowls. "Nope."

I shrug and go on eating. Poor kid, probably has a businessman father who is so intent on giving him all the right trappings — initials yet — that he doesn't even have a proper name. Could be what he's running away from.

But he surprises me. "I was really named after a person in the Bible. J, A, dash, E, L. People used to string it together so it sounded like 'Jail.' I didn't like that, so I decided I would go by my initials, J.L."

I haven't looked into a Bible for twenty years, so I nod and keep chewing. Religious parents. That makes sense. One small piece of information.

You never do hear too much about parents in the bush. The crew leave them well and properly behind. A good thing too, or I'd be thinking about my kids and where they are, without a father. Or if Janice has found them another one. That keeps me awake sometimes, when it's too quiet to sleep and I look up at the weave of the tent and think of them growing without me, never remembering me at all, thinking that I wasn't real. Or that I abandoned them.

Back in the hotel room, I sit down to work on the maps and airphotos, get the stratigraphy straight in my head, while the kid sits on the bed and swings one foot. It bothers me, him watching all the time.

"Why don't you make up a food order?" I say. "You better get all the basic stuff here because once we're out, the plane will only bring in weekly supplies."

He brightens and digs a pen out of that bulging knapsack. I hand him an order form and he sits for a while, chewing his nails. Finally he coughs. "Excuse me?"

"What?" I say, without looking up from my map.

"How many people will there be in camp?"

So he's not stupid. "Nine men. And you."

Half an hour later he has everything listed in neat rows in a square handwriting that is almost calligraphy. Too neat, I think, a cooktent littered with maps and rock samples is going to drive this guy crazy. But what can I do? I've hired him now and unless he serves us pork and beans five days in a row, I won't have any reason to fire him.

When I come out of the bathroom from brushing my teeth, he's already in bed, as if I've flashed a lights-out signal. He sleeps in his T-shirt, and that felt hat he hasn't removed all day is on the night-table beside him. He hasn't opened his pack either, just left it right in the corner where he dropped it. Doesn't even brush his teeth. Hell.

I kick my clothes into a heap and crawl into the other bed. I don't give a hang about assistants; I always sleep naked. That icy wetting hasn't helped my physical frame of mind and I feel like a long rest before I have to face Thompson and Jerome tomorrow. I only hope that cook doesn't keep me awake snoring; sometimes the little guys are worst of all.

Bill

You could tell something was up. He come helling in here like he was trailing a speedboat, and I swear I never seen Mackenzie so rattled in all the fifteen-odd years he's been coming up north.

"Bill," he says quick, "I need another Storm Haven."

Now, when it's May in Yellowknife and every company prospector and his dog has been through my store getting outfitted to hit the barrens and find a mine, I don't have a pumptent left, leave alone a Storm Haven.

I snort. "Mackenzie, if I had one I'd sell it to you, but a Storm Haven *now*? Hell, I even sold my kid's Boy Scout tent. I can sell you a tarp and some poles and pegs, that's about all I got left."

"Won't do," he says. "Won't do at all." And he looks around him to make sure no one's listening before he leans over the counter and says to me real soft, "Order me one from Edmonton special, okay? I'll pay for the extra cost. Just keep it quiet."

I blink and look at him. Maybe all those years of going up into that never-ending moss have finally softened his head. He's getting too old for it, a man should quit before he's forty. And I heard his wife left him, just walked out one day without leaving a hair to let him know where she'd gone.

"Mackenzie," I try to josh him a little. "You can double guys up for a while. I'll be getting another shipment in two weeks."

"Won't do," he says. "Come on, Bill, you'll get paid. I need that damn tent tomorrow."

So I find myself agreeing to phone down to Edmonton, where they think I've gone nuts.

"One Storm Haven, special shipment? Bill, can't this wait for your other order?"

I make some excuse and they're sure I'm crazy, but by the three o'clock plane the next day Mackenzie's got his Storm Haven.

Funniest thing. He heaves it into the back of that truck as if he's smashing rocks, madder'n hell. Well, I've seen all kinds go a little queer. Never expected it of him, sanest guy you could imagine and good for a few draft too, but then, you never can tell.

Mackenzie

It gave me the creeps. When I open one eye the next morning there he is, sitting on the edge of his barely rumpled bed, fully dressed, felt hat and all, swinging one booted foot and staring at me.

I get the feeling he's been watching me that way for a good half-hour or so, unblinking eyes on my unsuspecting face. I don't like it, the very idea wakes me up fast.

It isn't even late, just seven-thirty, and while I'm pulling on my clothes I can't get rid of this paranoid notion of him creeping around the room getting dressed, movements an exaggeration of quiet so he won't waken me. There is something about him that I can't place, even if he seems normal. Well, I could be overreacting. He hasn't done anything crazy. Maybe it's me and when the crew arrives he'll settle in. I'm just not used to having somebody around all the time.

I'm alone too much, they tell me. Mackenzie, stop mooning around that big house, get an apartment downtown, it's been ten years now. That startles me still. Sandy will be seventeen, and I might not recognize her. Ridiculous, of course I would — she's my kid, isn't she? I don't want to move, it's a good place, I like the trees we planted that spring when we bought it, the movers tracking mud from the new lawn all through the house and Stevie so excited falling down the basement steps. Stevie. My kid. I can't sell it. What if she came back and I wasn't there, a stranger at the door. I know Janice, it would kill her resolution, she'd never try again.

It's mornings when I think of them most. I'm still not used to waking in an empty house, no sound or movement anywhere. Evenings I can concentrate on papers and maps, my collection. So maybe it's me and not the cook, I don't know what kids his age are like anymore. Every year the crew seems a little more removed from me, a little younger.

Whatever he is, he's not lazy. We rumble through the warehouse digging out equipment hastily abandoned last fall when everyone was helling to get home and he heaves and pulls and sorts with me quite cheerfully, as if he's easier with movement, doing something. Even so, bending over a dusty Coleman lantern, there is something in the flicker of his hands that bothers me, leaves me with a vague remembrance I cannot place, almost like a smell. And that felt hat practically glued to his head.

We get all the stuff stacked in neat piles so that the crew can load it and haul it to the dock, and I have to admit the kid doesn't mind working at all. Some of them would rather talk than do anything, but this one lights into the job with a steady concentration and only stops now and then to take a bite at his nails or to jam that hat tighter on his head.

So I'm a little surprised when he hitches his chair toward me and says uneasily, "Hey, Mackenzie, I've got to talk to you." This is a sure bet for confession and since this kid has barely said a word so far I almost edge away. I always expect the worst now. One kid backed me into a corner and sheepishly told me he'd invited his aunt to come and visit him in the bush. I didn't worry, figured he didn't mean it or that she couldn't find us anyway, but a month later there she was in a floatplane loaded with chocolate cake and red wine. Figured those were two things poor little nephew couldn't get in the bush. The wine was great but I had a hell of a time persuading her that she couldn't stay for the rest of the summer. As for the kid, the crew forever after called him "poor nephew" and made his summer long and miserable. Rich kids shouldn't become geologists.

But there we are, bending back a few in the middle of Yellowknife's only draft-serving bar, bending back a few — and I notice approvingly that the kid does drink beer — when he hitches his chair and coughs and says in that scratchy half-voice of his, "Hey, Mackenzie, I've got to talk to you."

"What is it?" And all of a sudden I'm apprehensive as hell. What's eating this kid anyway?

He looks around, then suddenly says, "I gotta go to the can," shoves back his chair and practically runs off. I get up and follow him. I can't hold nearly as much as I used to and sometimes it seems I spend almost as much time standing in front of a bar's urinal as I do bending my elbow. He's in a cubicle, so I position myself and arch my back in enormous release. "What's bugging you?" I say into the booming enamel. Why is it that no matter how dirty a washroom is, it still seems to echo? Of course, clean ones echo most.

The toilet flushes and he comes out of the cubicle and stands beside me and stares at my cock singing piss against the enamel. Now, there's one thing. It's bad manners to stare. All cocks are more or less the same when they're not stiff, and this kid is holding that felt hat with one hand and looking at me like he's never even seen one before. I'm beginning to think that his problem is he's queer, when he says flat out and still staring at my member, "Mackenzie, I'm a girl."

Zeke

I never seen the like of it. I've been sitting by this door watching this bar for years, watching and watching the black-stockinged waitresses swinging their loaded trays through the crush of tables and workboots, watching the pretty little girls turn into whores, watching the whores get picked up by the road crews and the miners and geologists, watching for the glint of a knife or a razor, watching for laughter, watching for the rumble of a percolating fight. I seen everything here. I've seen people get killed and people make love and, yes, one woman even had a baby in here. Popped it in the corner right next to the jukebox. The floor has soaked up so much sweat and smoke and beer that it's rotting underneath and one day the whole building will collapse.

They don't trust me, maybe because I'm Déné, maybe because I never drink. I just sit here on this high stool by the door and watch. I'm a big man, really big, and there's one rule. If you fight, you hit the sidewalk.

But I seldom see a man run out of here leaving a tableful of beer behind. I know Mackenzie, he's been coming here for years, party chief for some big outfit and a decent guy, always says hello to me, always polite, never crazy like some. But he streaks out of that can like a rousted tom, grabs his jacket and just about tears the door off getting out. I'm on my way to check the can — maybe it's on fire — when out comes the funny-looking little guy in the felt hat he's been drinking with. I grab his arm and he turns and snarls at me without a word, and I'm damned if sure enough it's not a girl. Only women can look mad like that.

"Hey, you keep your ass out of the men's."

She only blares those eyes at me, the funniest little thing, straight and flat as a boy, blue jeans and boots and short cropped hair under an old soft hat. Only her eyes and the corners of her mouth show she's a girl. She shakes me off and stomps out without a word. I never seen the like. Mackenzie's got himself a bear trap.

J.L.

I knew that if I put down my name, J.L., and left the sex, F for female, box unchecked, they would assume I was a man. Only one gender has initials, the rest of us are misses and mistresses with neither the dignity of anonymity nor the prestige of assumption. All men are equal.

I did it deliberately. I wanted this job, I wanted to head for nowhere and look at everything in my narrow world from a detached distance. I wanted it so much that for weeks I schemed, I lay awake concocting ways to get here without lying. I thought that my initials would get me past first scrutiny, but I didn't even count on their unassailable arrogance, that even if I left the sex box empty, no "F" or "M" to delineate, it didn't matter. Women don't steal male conventions. They must have noticed, but assumed it was masculine carelessness on my part. Initials stand for a man.

My experience is good, my letter of reference from the hotel calls me J.L. and does not refer to me as "she" at all. I am not surprised when the official letter tendering the job of camp cook arrives. I carry that letter around in my pocket until it is rubbed limp, slide my fingers across it in boring classes on mores, a patch of heat against my skin, the promise of aloneness. With that name, *Mackenzie*, that explorer's name in an illegible scrawl at the bottom of the page. I can think only of taking myself away, separating from all my myriad and tedious connections.

Jamsie, after all, gave me the idea. He was one of them, lovers I mean, one of the countless fetters. He catches me out at an uneven moment when I am crouched behind a stack of books, thinking myself safe.

"J.L.! I've been calling you for weeks!" Accusing voice.

I raise my face to his assuming smile, then look down at the open book on my knees. Freud. I sometimes feel I must refresh my dislikes.

"I've been staying at a friend's."

"Why didn't you let me know?"

I get to my feet and deliberately put the book back in its numbered place. "Jamsie, did it ever occur to you that I didn't want to?"

His eyes widen, hurt. "If you'd just say something, J.L. . . . "

"It takes too much effort." I fan my hand at the sober lines of books. "I've been here, how many years? We all hide here, see each other every day, stick up for each other in seminars, screw each other after class, graduate students à la — It makes me sick."

He makes a gesture of disgust. "Ah, J.L., why don't you go live on an island? You've always felt you were too damn good for the rest of us. Why don't you go live in the Arctic? Who would miss you?"

He pouts away around the corner of the stack, a weedy, absentminded man who could forget what he was doing in the middle of making love. I think he secretly liked boys, not women, and I was a compromise. Maybe women express something innate when we choose truck drivers or farmers; they do not carry their apparatus so self-consciously as academics do, always.

But there it was, the idea. The Arctic is so close to here, so immediate that it throws a heavy shadow across this city. I'm surprised I didn't think of it myself.

I hunt up Paul, a geology graduate who has given up bushwork for controlled laboratory experiments in a dark basement room piled high with core boxes, everywhere boxes and burlap bags.

"Can you cook?" He is peering into a microscope.

"Of course I can cook. I even spent one summer job in a hotel kitchen. I was born knowing how to cook!"

"Apply as a cook then," he says to the black tube. "But don't get your hopes up. Most outfits don't like to hire women." He adjusts the focus, bends forward eagerly as if he is on the verge of a discovery. "Common theory is it's bad for camp morale."

24

I snort. "Surely you mean morals."

He lifts his head and then swivels away from the microscope, puts on his glasses as if everything should be seen through a lens. "No. Morale."

"You don't think it's a good idea, do you?"

He shrugs, already turned halfway back to the microscope. "Depends. Depends who the party chief is, what the crew is like, who really runs the camp. You get some strange guys up there. Running around the barrens, hammering at outcrops, walking ten miles with fifty pounds of worthless rocks on their back. I knew a couple of guys who didn't carry rock hammers. They carried sledgehammers. Every time they'd see a boulder they'd pound it to pieces, hooting and hollering as if every lump of granite was gold. Crazy."

He is getting a permanent slouch from bending over that microscope. "Where do you get your samples?" I ask sarcastically.

He waves a vague hand. "There are always rocks around here. Look at this place. Those boxes are full of rocks, samples, suites from expeditions, mine tours, reconnaissance camps. Nobody wants them, they've forgotten they're here. I've got enough samples to last me a lifetime."

"What are you looking at now?"

And even though his face is screwed up against the eyepiece, I can see his happy smile. "The crystal structure of ruby-red sphalerite," he says. "Perfection itself."

Jerome

I knew something would go wrong. I never worked with the man before, but I've watched him enough to know. He's too soft, he shouldn't be out in the bush anymore, he's over forty, I'm sure. I knew when they told me I would be working with him, he'll be the party chief and I'll do all the work. I've been out ten years, it should be my program, I know far more than he does about uranium, far more than he does about the area. And he's stubborn, won't listen to me, just nods and does what he's going to do. Well, this summer should be his last. Why else would they put us on a program together?

But it's worse than I expected. When Thompson and I get off the plane from Edmonton, he's waiting for us with a look on his face like he just swallowed something nasty. He's been in the bar, I can smell beer. I ask him about our plans right away, but he just ignores me and starts helping Thompson with map tubes and the radio box. He hasn't learned to let the assistants do the shitwork, that's all they're good for. Like Thompson. If you don't get after him he'll wander around theorizing forever. And dumb ideas, the guy thinks he's living in a science fiction movie. He's been in geology for eight years, but he's got no drive, no instinct for success, doesn't run, doesn't keep up with hockey, talks to the secretaries in the office, goes to the symphony with his screwy girlfriend. I bet he even smokes dope.

In some ways Mackenzie and him remind me of each other. Mackenzie's been coming up here for fifteen, twenty years now, and never made it into management. Sure, he found a crummy mine, but it never got him anywhere. Besides, there's something wrong with a man who can't control his wife, who lets her walk out the door on him. Shirley ought to try it, she'd find out fast. But then, she wouldn't in the first place, she's got respect.

Mackenzie tells us that the cook's here already and the rest of the crew come in tomorrow, so if the breakup cooperates, we'll be out soon. I always hate the beginning of the summer. Nobody's organized, the crew's getting drunk and carrying on, assistants have to be trained. They can't seem to settle down until they've been out for a week and they're looking at three months of unbroken tundra. I run a dry camp, but who knows what Mackenzie will let them get away with.

We meet in his hotel room to take a quick look at the maps. Our target areas are good. We could have a successful summer. Mackenzie has an idea up his sleeve; he insists that we're not to tell the rest of the crew where we're going. Maybe he's catching on; I never tell the crew a damn thing. And then there's a knock on the door.

"It's the cook," says Mackenzie. He stands up and I hardly have time to blink before he's saying, as if he's been rehearsing all night, "I'd like you to meet J.L. We're very lucky she's going to cook for us this summer." His face is as studiously blank as if he has wiped it clean with a cloth.

I look from him to her and back again, can hardly believe he is serious. She's a girl, flat-chested as they come, but a girl. And now I know he's really flipped out of line. Thompson is grinning like a fool and shaking her hand, he isn't old enough to know a thing about women. Got wierd ideas, why he once told me that he thought female geologists worked harder than men. Far as I'm concerned, they shouldn't even let them into geology, it's a man's field.

"And this is Jerome. He's assistant party chief," Mackenzie says. Goddamn him.

She nods at me, turns back to Mackenzie. "Breakfast at eight?"

"Fine," he says. "See you then."

"Goodnight." At the door she looks over her shoulder and grins at Thompson as if she's known him for years.

"Do you know her?" I say to him.

He laughs. "Never seen her before in my life."

Mackenzie is leaning over the maps. "All right, if we concentrate on this area first — "

"Wait a minute! What the fuck is going on here?"

"What do you mean?" says Mackenzie, eyeing me cool as you please.

"A goddamn girl?"

Thompson has a grin on his face that's as wide as the tundra. "She looks pretty good to me," he says.

I ignore him, his opinion doesn't count. "You can't have a girl in camp. She won't be able to stand the isolation, she'll be nothing but trouble."

"Why?" says Mackenzie.

"One girl and a bunch of men? You've gone crazy!"

"Why?" he says again in that quiet voice of his.

"Jesus! Come on, Mackenzie, you know it will never work!"

He just looks at me, his eyes getting harder and bluer. Like I said, stubborn, but I've got to talk him out of making a big mistake.

"Do you mean to tell me that you actually decided to hire that girl to cook?"

"Well," he says, "not exactly."

"The little bitch roped you into it."

"No," he says softly, "I hired her."

"Fire her."

He almost smiles. "What for?"

"Company policy, camp rules, think of something. She can't do anything about it. Mackenzie, it's impossible to work in a camp with a girl. It's bad for morale."

He stares at me for a long time, clenching and unclenching his hands. Thompson's grin is wiped off his face and he looks from Mackenzie to me and back again. Then Mackenzie turns and slowly and carefully begins to roll up one of the maps.

"Jerome, I understand your feelings, but if you don't like having a woman in camp, perhaps you should ask to be put on another program. You're behaving like a schoolboy who wrinkles up his nose and says, 'Girls. Ugh, germs!' She may be a woman, but I won't fire her. She is going to cook for us this summer."

He has gone crazy. "You know what the company thinks about it!"

Carefully he slides the rolled-up map into a tube. "I know what the company thinks about women in the bush. I'll answer for her."

Trust somebody like him. I won't stand for it, she'll ruin the summer. Besides, she'll never last. Women just don't belong out there. I wonder how she did it, what kind of deal she made with him. A little young to be his girlfriend, but then you can't tell anymore. Besides, girls like her will screw anybody to get what they want.

Mackenzie

I'm not a superstitious man. If I were, I would have quit geology long ago. Some men think that if a summer starts wrong, it will be bad until it's over. I've never believed that, but now I'm beginning to wonder.

She surprised me, threw me off balance. Not that she's a woman but that I didn't recognize it, didn't see it even after two days and a night with her right under my chin. I must be losing touch, any other man would have smelled her. She does look some like a boy, Thompson said that right off. But it's one thing for her to look like a boy and quite another for me to honestly believe, for no less than two days, that she *is* a boy. That hat helped. When she took it off and I had a chance to study her, I could see even the shape of her head is female. Probably why she kept it on, clamped onto it like that. Once I'd made the mistake, she wasn't sure how to tell me. When she finally did, I knew instantly and without doubt it was what I'd been worrying at, and that realization jolted me. Oh, it wasn't that I'd somehow hired a woman, but that I'd literally mistaken her for a man.

Janice left me ten years ago and since then I can easily count the number of women I've touched. The women I saw as women, sex, not secretaries or friends' wives or colleagues or just women walking, moving, sitting, women on the bus and at the grocery store. And suddenly I realize that I haven't had a woman for three years. I can hardly believe myself, surely I must be forgetting, but no, I remember every one.

I remember Janice so clearly. When she'd been gone a while I tried hookers, easy enough to arrange, but they were never quite right, something always distracted me. I would look for one that resembled her, her height or her kind of hair, but it felt as if by screwing them I was trying to change her and I never wanted to do that. Then I started spending an occasional evening with Hélène, a little French girl who worked in the drafting department. I was just getting used to her when one day she exploded, said I was a nice man but too damn absentminded to notice anything. I honestly don't know what she was talking about. She threw me out of her west-end apartment so quick I was standing in the hall before I realized what had happened. We never went to my house.

Six months later she married one of the geophysicists and only stopped outside my office door one day to say, "See? Are you happy now?"

I don't understand what I did wrong. I liked her fine but in some ways it was easier to go back to the hookers, didn't have to pretend anything with them, just do it and go out empty. Until I only picked one up every six months or so. I felt sad for them, those girls huddled in doorways getting tired feet and looking at you so anxiously when you walked past, pretending so hard not to care. And some of them were young; well, it felt like I was their father and I couldn't take that.

But to think I haven't done it for three years?

And then Jerome. I didn't expect I would like him much, but I figured he'd be decent. Turns out he's more fanatic about the rules and the way things get done than he ever showed in the office, at least that I noticed. I wouldn't have predicted it. He always seemed reasonable. Of course, it was the cook that set him off. I know I'll end up having to keep him away from her. If I won't fire her, he'll make life so miserable that she'll probably quit.

The only thing makes me chuckle is, she's tough. Behind that soft mouth of hers she's like a quick little snake, the kind you don't see until after they've bitten you. He starts on her that first morning at breakfast. I wonder if I should interfere, lay the law down to him once and for all, but after a minute I just eat my eggs and pretend not to listen.

"If you're the cook," he says to her before she even has a chance for a swallow of coffee, "what are your qualifications?"

He's eating and talking at the same time in that nervous, aggressive way of his, elbows stuck out and glaring at her across the table.

She starts to eat, calmly chews and swallows a mouthful before she says a word. "One summer working in a hotel and ten years cooking for threshing crews. Say," she leans toward him confidentially, "think you can eat as much as a prairie thresher?"

That's when I figure I don't have to worry about her. He looks a little put out, but it makes him mad that she dares to lip him.

"It's not quantity I'm concerned about," he says disdainfully.

"Oh, you want to know my specialties? Beef Bourguignon, Chicken Kiev, Côte de Veau aux Champignons, Scallopine à la Vongole, Medaillons du porc, clam chowder so thick it can climb a ladder and curry so tantalizing it will make your tongue burn just to smell it. Of course, I prefer the Ukrainian method of making bread, the Oriental method for vegetables, the German method for soups, and there is nothing to equal Italian torte!"

Thompson is practically falling off his chair and I have to swallow some toast to hide my smile. Jerome gets a little redder than he is already. "Too damn spicy. Guys in the bush want meat and potatoes."

She heaves an audible sigh. "How disappointing. Well, I can certainly manage something that simple. By the way, did you say you had an ulcer?"

"No!" he barks. "I just hate spicy food!"

She takes a dainty bite of toast. "Lack of experience," she says airily. "You have to develop a taste for these things." And she smiles at him like he's a little boy who simply won't eat carrots.

He has a look in his eyes as if he would gladly strangle her on the spot. "I've got plenty of experience. But my wife is the only woman I've ever met who can cook worth a damn!"

Thompson can't resist himself. "Jerome, you should have brought her along."

But I'm watching J.L. and that's when I see the snake in her undulate, just a shade. Jerome doesn't see it, or surely he'd have the sense to let her alone. She faces his scarlet fury with a look like lucid ice. "Jerome," she says, laying her knife and fork correctly, so precisely across her plate. "I can cook dishes that you don't even know how to pronounce." She rises. "Excuse me, gentlemen, I have work to do today." And walks away, leaving Jerome spluttering over his now-cold scrambled eggs.

"See," he flings at me, "see? The little bitch is going to be nothing but trouble!"

"Gee," says Thompson innocently. "Sure sounds like she can cook."

Jerome whirls on him. "Don't you step out of line, Thompson. Who gives a fuck if she can cook?"

Thompson hoots with laughter. "I thought that's why we hired her!"

Jerome may try to kill her before the summer is over, but it seems we'll be entertained.

As if that isn't enough, I'm sitting in my room after breakfast making a checklist for the day when the phone rings. I figure it's Jerome crazy to get going, so I take my time answering, but it's P.Q. from the office.

"Mackenzie," he says, "we've got a problem."

I don't say a word but my gut tells me that if I thought I had trouble before, this could be the end of my summer. Like I said, I don't believe in bad luck, but once it gets rolling, seems like it's hard to stop.

"Mackenzie, are you there?"

"Yeah sure. What's up?"

"Well, I hate to be the one to have to tell you this, but there's a hot area opened up in the Wernecke mountains, just across the Yukon border. We got a private prospector's report a while ago and it looks like a sure bet for uranium.

We have to send a major reconnaissance camp in there right now and since you're our senior uranium man, you're it."

Shit. The Yukon mountains. It's not just the climbing, they must be crazy if they think we'll find enough uranium there to make the scint beep once.

"What about my program?"

"We'll send somebody else after it."

Somebody else will find my mine. And suddenly I'm mad. "You're not giving it to Jerome?"

He laughs. "No. Jerome goes with you."

"And I want Thompson and my cook."

"You can take your original crew. We're sending you a helicopter, Jet Ranger, pilot with an engineer's license. He should arrive there today."

"But what about my program?"

"Listen, Mackenzie, I'm sorry. Graham's crew will spend a month there at the end of summer."

"A month for a three-month program? I was going to find a mine there!"

"You can find a mine where you're going. Mackenzie, I know it's sudden, but the area is hot and you're the only man who has the experience to walk into a uranium patch unprepared. You should have seen the samples this guy had!"

"Hasn't anybody checked it out?"

"I flew in and had a look at it last week. It needs work but it looks good. The money got approved yesterday, you've got $300,000. We've considered a program there for three years and every year we put it off. Now we can't wait any longer or this guy will go to the competition and we'll be beaten out."

P.Q. couldn't recognize a uranium deposit if it zapped him between the legs. But I go where I'm told. "What can I say?"

"Thanks, Mackenzie, I knew I could count on you. I've sent the background material, maps, assay results on the samples, by registered mail. You should get it all today."

"Can I at least assay for other minerals?"

He laughs. "Sure. Nobody will object if you find silver. Don't be so glum, Mackenzie, it's beautiful country. Wish I was coming with you."

But you're not, I think. Good old P.Q. He knew when to get out of the leg work. Not that much older than me either. Maybe it's time I started to think about staying in the office. Smack in the middle of the Yukon mountains, contouring those slopes all summer. Like I said, seems there's no end to bad luck once it starts.

J.L.

When he zipped himself up and bolted out of the men's I figured my summer was over. Why did I have to blurt it out there, in an awkward place like that? My conscience again, I can't restrain it.

I thought he would figure it out, catch on to me. But after that first night I knew that the idea of me being a woman hadn't even occurred to him. And what's more, it wouldn't, not unless I told him.

What could I do? I could hardly act out that charade all summer. So there we are in the bar having a few rounds and I'm hoping the beer will unveil some way to approach the subject, when I get this uncontrollable urge to urinate. It makes me uncomfortable right away, I can't follow through on confessing I'm a girl when my bladder is aching, so I stand and say, "I gotta go to the can."

And instantly realize what I've done. The women's is on one side of the bar and the men's is on the other. Which one do I use? If I go to the women's, I'll be choosing a slanted way of telling him, and somehow I have a feeling I should be direct. Besides, judging from the last two days, he's not likely to even notice. But the men's. . . It's my only alternative, I have to play this straight until I can tell him. I hope to hell they've got cubicles with doors here.

They do. One. I lock myself in and get rid of an hour's accumulation of beer, still mulling over what I'm going to say to him. I hear someone come in and unzip, stand in front of the urinal. I'll just have to stay in here until he leaves. Then Mackenzie's voice says, "What's bugging you?"

You know why it's hard to tell him? I like him. He's quiet, he's sensible, he doesn't try to corner a person. I don't want him to change the way he treats me. He's a good man, he likes himself, he likes what he does, he isn't interested in holding you down. And it's not that he's been converted, he's just innocent. So innocent and unaware I think he can't be serious, but he is. I hate to disappoint him, but I can't keep this up.

And I can't sit in here and say nothing, let his question suspend itself in the fetid air. Men's washrooms smell of urine; they haven't been taught to be so damned antiseptic about their excrement as we women have. I flush the toilet noisily and walk out.

He's standing in front of the urinal, relaxed, calmly aiming at the stained enamel, expecting me to tell him I have a toothache or that I miss my girlfriend. I look at him, an average man with brown hair and blue eyes, about forty but in good shape, a normal ordinary man with a wife and two kids I'm sure, with a suburban house and a stationwagon. He has a nice cock too, I can see, shapely, not long, a neat circumcision. But what am I thinking of, standing here staring at him, and what can I do but answer his question.

"Mackenzie, I'm a girl."

That was bad, not subtle at all. I haven't given him any of the preamble I intended, haven't explained myself like I planned.

I follow him back to the hotel, thinking of the barren-lands, that shivering silence stretched out over the pale flatness, treeless and unashamed. If he's not angry, he's at least upset. But am I really that indistinct? I've never been taken for a man before, although I sometimes wish I were one. It seems so much simpler for them, everything is clearcut, laid out from the moment they're born. They do not have the questions and doubts that get laid on our backs, the bundle of faggots we carry and carry. I've tried to throw it off, fling it on the ground and abandon it, but although I sometimes lose a stick or two, the weight is still there, old myths and old lovers, old duties, my mother's warning voice, my infallible conscience.

I do look somewhat like a boy. It's a disguise rather than a denial. It's useful to be small and thin and flat. It saves me from myself, hides my openness to hurt. Men are more likely to be first attracted to my head and what I say. And they always express amazement at my desire, as if my kind of body should not be capable of it.

Deborah is the opposite, as lush as I am spare. And although I've sometimes thought I would gladly trade my bundle for hers, when I see the way men move toward her I can be happy with my own. We've been friends for years, truly friends, trading our secrets and confessions unfailingly. For years I've watched men lunge at her, unable to control their hands, reaching for a strand of her hair, watching for the slightest movement of her wide mouth. And they're always surprised, oh she surprises them, a woman with a profane body that is underneath as cold as steel; surprised to find, when they reach for that softness, a trap, a brain as uncompromising as her body seems inviting. Oh, she's made me understand, I can be happy with myself, rejoice in what I lack. For I have seen her weep, seen the slow tears dripping between the fingers covering her siren's face. And I have heard her curse herself, curse the lovely prison of her limbs. And even I, in secret longing to be like her, can barely understand; why would anyone not want to be beautiful?

But I have never masqueraded as a boy.

I will explain it all to him, tell him how much I want to go, how much I want to hear silence. I am so tired of confessions. But I'm afraid that Paul was right. Women mean trouble, and I haven't exactly started things off very well. I'm sure Mackenzie'll ship me back to Edmonton on the first plane tomorrow morning.

The door to the room is open and through it I see him hunched over his spread maps, studying them as if they could reveal something, as if they might protect him. Those maps seem to chart an outline for his life; he handles them so carefully, so lovingly, refers to them again and again. Looking at him there, the outline of his face and shoulder, the inherent strength of the forearm laid across the desk, I want suddenly to touch him, to comfort him for all the unmapped areas, to tell him how truly sorry I am that I cannot stay a boy.

"Don't stand outside the door," he says without raising his head or looking at me. "Come in."

I walk into the room and shut the door.

He studies the map as if it will help him think of words to say.

"Are you going to fire me?" I wait. I will not apologize for being a woman.

He follows the course of a river with his pencil. "Can you cook?"

I blink, his logic is surprising. "Yes, I can cook."

Then he swivels in the chair and studies me for a moment, forehead creased under untidy hair that I can see will be gray in a few years. "I mean," he says slowly, "can you really *cook*?"

I begin to understand. He is embarrassed at himself, upset that he has mistaken me for a boy, but now that we are staring at each other, I know he doesn't want to fire me, he doesn't give a damn whether I'm a man or a woman.

I move toward him and reach out my hand. "Mackenzie, I promise you I'll be the best damn cook you've ever had."

He takes my hand and holds it for a moment as if measuring my strength. "Not a word, hear?"

I nod.

He grins then and I realize I have not had to explain. He knows.

"Oh," he shakes his pencil at me. "It won't be easy, they're not used to it, they won't like it."

I only smile at him until he fidgets.

"Well, you've got your way," he says gruffly. "Let's get you another room before I go out to the airport to pick up Thompson and Jerome."

Thompson

The night before we leave we hit the bar. One last glorious smash. We're all here now getting ready for the summer, Cap and Hearne and Franklin starting early with me so that by eight o'clock the walls are blurred and we've forgotten about supper. Later Mackenzie shows up with that weird kid and Jerome's assistant, and Ivan, our newly requisitioned helicopter pilot. Even Jerome appears and has a few draft — right decent of him since we paid.

Hearne patiently explains camera lenses to the kid, Milton, who won't drink beer but will down whopping amounts of tomato juice to keep us company. Franklin is demonstrating the proper posture for meditation, and Cap has his chair tipped back and his eyes closed as he snaps his fingers along with the jukebox when all of a sudden my head jerks up and I glare at Mackenzie.

"Where's the cook?"

Across the table, Mackenzie takes a reflective drink. "In the hotel, I guess. Didn't want to drink."

I try to focus on his face, so that I can make sure he's not lying. Mackenzie can't lie worth a damn. I point at him accusingly. "You fired her."

"No, she's coming."

Cap blinks and looks at Mackenzie. "She? Who?"

He is almost ready to pass out, but if Cap even hears a feminine pronoun he sobers up fast.

Mackenzie grins. "Nobody. You're all drunk."

I shake my head. "Uh uh. I saw her. I saw her. Twice."

Mackenzie takes another swallow of beer. "Had your eyes checked lately?"

"I did! Just ask Jerome — " and I turn to him but Jerome is gone, the chair is empty.

Mackenzie lifts his hand for another round. "Thompson, you're hallucinating."

"Hey, don't you try to shit me. I *saw* her, I *talked* to her!"

"Did you touch her?" His face is absolutely straight except that it keeps doubling and tripling on me.

I close my eyes in an effort to remember and suddenly I'm not so sure. This is like the beginning of every field season, and every other field season never had any girl before.

"I shure. . . I shook hands. . . "

Mackenzie laughs aloud. "Thompson, you're drunk!"

I pound my fist on the table so everyone will listen. "Hey, you guys! You saw 'er. The cook."

They all look at me like I'm crazy and then go on drinking. Cap reaches over to pat my shoulder. "Come on, Thompson. Stop dreamin'! They'd never give us a girl and you know it."

I slump in my chair and stare at the littered table. "I did so see 'er."

Mackenzie laughs again.

"You lyin' bastard," I growl. "You're tryin' 'a mix me up."

"You're already mixed up," Mackenzie says. "Don't you think so, Zeke?" He grins up at that big native bouncer who is suddenly there beside our table. "Look at these guys, Zeke. Blind drunk. You oughta throw them out."

"Last night, eh?" Zeke grunts. "How come you stay sober, Mac?" Zeke is the only guy who ever calls Mackenzie Mac.

"I got work to do tonight."

Zeke looks down at Mackenzie and I might have been drunk, but I know he moved his lips in the closest thing to a smile that anyone's ever seen him give.

"You gonna bait it or spring it?"

"What?" says Mackenzie.

"That bear trap."

"What bear trap?"

Zeke snorts and claps one huge hand on Mackenzie's shoulder before he turns back to his post at the door. "Have a good summer," he says before even he becomes a blur.

Mackenzie

From here the cold surface of the water reflects inlaid turquoise against a dull overhang of mountains. You might believe that the ice has melted but it's only sunk, green and congealed, to the bottom of the lake where it will hover all summer, chilling the water. That damn lake will never be warm enough to swim in.

The snow too lies scattered and torn in patches on the moss. In between, our boxes and bags, our summer's survival, seems lost, inadequate.

We're here. The middle of the Wernecke mountains in an alpine valley that never feels summer, just varying shades of winter. Nothing to break the angry gusts coming off those mountains. We're above tree line, above everything, it seems. I'm still thinking about the barrens and my abandoned program, but what can I do about that now? We're here.

The wind carries the sound of ourselves away, thins the voices of the crew setting up the Storm Havens, clustered close together as if to ward off the same chill I feel. Behind me the big white Jutland stands stretched and solid but does not break the shrill keen of the wind through the watery sunlight. And then I hear the distant *whump whump whump* of the helicopter rotor slicing air, and even before the Jet Ranger roars over the slate-gray ridge to the east we're all standing hammer-in-hand looking up. Above the crest it seems to hesitate, then plummets down in a spiral of yellow and black, blades singing now above the wind. I run to the level ground behind the Jutland, wave my arms in a circle to signal a flat landing spot. The crew still stands face up, open-mouthed. In the cockpit I catch a flash of the pilot's sunglasses beside Thompson's grinning face.

The machine needles closer and closer to the ground, dust and dry winter moss blowing up from the cushion of air under the skids, when suddenly the Storm Havens billow and lift, struggle olive and canvas and alive against their puny ropes and pegs. Through the alarmed cries of the running crew and the whirl of the blades, the six tents rise one by one. Huge crippled kites, they green the chilly air like blossoming sails for one wild escaped moment, only to hesitate and then collapse in heaps of inert canvas on the gray moss. The white Jutland alone stands unshivered and solid. The motor screams one last time and then falls away to a slow wail that lengthens into a sigh, blades still turning *swish swish swish swish* in the after-quiet of the throttled wind. For a moment everything is still, and then, hat on her head, wooden spoon in her hand, J.L. steps through the flap of that still-standing Jutland — her cooktent — and starts to laugh. She laughs loud and wide at the lumpy heaps of tents.

The pilot eyes her sourly. "It's not funny. Damn dangerous if one of those got caught in the blades."

But the crew is already re-erecting the tents farther away, cursing and laughing as if the summer has been announced. J.L. is talking to them, her voice carries down between the *tap tap tap* of a hammer on an iron tent peg.

They surprise me. I thought her presence would stifle the crew, hamper them some, at least until they got used to her, but they seem determined to act as if she's a common occurrence, something they encounter every summer. All of them falling over each other to pretend she's nothing special. But I can see the wheels, every one of them planning how long it will take to sneak into her tent.

Now it feels as if we are here, that chill wind doesn't matter a damn, the summer has started. And maybe if Thompson doesn't mind supervising camp chores, I can take that goddamn chopper and get up on that mountain and see if there really is anything here.

Milton

Not one Christian.

The cook is a girl. They said there weren't any girls up north.

Ivan

Since they phoned me and told me I was coming up here, I haven't had time to piss. Course, it's the kind of job I was waiting for. A whole summer's flying will really build up my hours. Nice little machine too. I'd rather fly a 206 B than a Hiller or a Bell 47 any day. And I guess I was what they were looking for. Hard to find a guy who's both a pilot and an engineer. Sure helps a man to land jobs if he doesn't have much experience. This summer should log me some two hundred-odd hours and with that I can fly wherever I want. It's the guys with the hours who get the cushy jobs flying pipeline and spraying. They never spend three months in the Yukon mountains.

But what the hell, it's all experience. Party chief seems like a good man, quiet and easy. He won't give me any trouble. That other sour-faced bastard does nothing but give orders. Nobody listens. Except the skinny English kid who must be his assistant or something. Poor sucker. He's gonna have himself a summer. And when I find out that the cook is a girl, the summer brightens up in a hurry. Funny, but it seems like camps that have women in them are more relaxed, easygoing. Guys don't get so hostile, so foul-mouthed, as they do if they see nothing but men for three months. Not so daredevil either, and let me tell you, that makes it a lot easier on the chopper pilot's life insurance. Get a bunch of men talking and pretty soon they want to start doing stunts, taking bomber dives from the sky.

Besides, one thing is sure. The food will be better. Never forget that old bastard last summer. He'd cook all right, but he'd never eat with us. He'd just sit there and watch us eat, chuckling a little now and then. Got so I could hardly force it down, with him sitting there watching and nodding his head and smiling. Got to the point where you weren't sure what you were eating. So one day I grabbed him and shook him, threatened to kill him if he didn't tell us what he'd done to the stew. But he swore up and down he hadn't done a thing, just made ordinary stew. The party chief stopped me from hammering his head in. But he still wouldn't eat with us. Just watched and chuckled. Boy, I had one uneasy stomach. Anything would be an improvement on that.

The day after I hit Yellowknife we're ready to leave. Half the crew and the equipment fly out in a Twin Otter, guess there's a lake there. Jerome and his British assistant and another guy wait for the second trip, the fuel and the radio and the antennaes. I can tell he doesn't like setting up camp.

Thompson flies in with me, navigates. He seems like a cheerful sort. Can tell right away he likes to fly. Has that look on his face when we lift off the pad like a kid at the circus. And sure enough, I find out he's got a private pilots' license, flies light aircraft as often as he can. Asks me questions about the chopper all the way. What's more, doesn't get us lost. Navigates straight to that camp site, all the while I'm trying to figure out where the hell we're going. I would've gotten lost, those damn lakes all look the same.

And then I'm easing that chopper flat against the cross-wind, trying to set her down gentle and even, when every goddamn one of those half-staked tents takes off like a kite in a storm. Christ. I just hang onto the stick and pray. All you need is one tarp to get caught in a blade and *crash*, you're dead. Good thing they're anchored and they just blow over.

But when I step out and duck my head for the blades, walk over to Mackenzie, who says, "Welcome to Fort Chaos," all I can think is, what the hell am I doing here?

Mackenzie

All crew on camp construction.

1. Pitch tents, tarps.

2. Set up antennaes. Have Cap check radio contact.

3. Build table, drafting board, shelves, stand for stove in cooktent.

4. Build shower.

5. Dig garbage pit.

6. Dig latrine.

7. Dig pit for meat locker.

8. Study airphotos.

9. Get maps sorted.

10. Figure out budget allotment.

Thompson

Even with a hangover, the ride in the chopper is something, better than any airplane. It's as if we hang suspended over these mountains, the blades cradling us, hardly seeming to advance against the endless peaks below. Effortlessly, the chopper rises to clear a ridge and just over, drops full throttle to plummet to the sweep of the valley floor. That climb, that marvelous and never-ending fall, is like a magic roller coaster that rides the contours of the mountains. Maybe I can convince Ivan to let me try flying this machine. It's harder to fly a chopper than an airplane, I know; keeping it on a balance with that heavy stick between your knees takes concentration and strength. Ivan is such a little guy, he doesn't seem that strong. But he loves to fly, I can tell by the way he settles in his seat and revs the motor until the blades sing, by the skim of that lift and turn when he pulls the chopper into the air.

Mackenzie is not happy about this place, but I am. We are camped on a cirque beside a lake, the perfect location, too high for bugs. We'll be here all summer. I can hardly wait to get up on that ridge and start scouting, the outcrops here are so much better than on the barrenlands. But today we'll set up camp. Mackenzie leaves me in charge while he takes the helicopter up to check out the claims we've optioned. I don't mind. Of course Jerome has arranged it so he comes in on the last plane, he won't do the shitwork.

I kneel on the plywood floor of the Jutland hammering crossed two by fours together so that the table will be steady, a trestle. I like carpentering, making pieces of wood into something real and usable. Outside, the voices of the crew punctuate my hammer.

"Where's the goddamn line?"

"Hey, Cap, bring that extra shovel, will you?"

By tonight the camp will be a place, the cooktent in the center facing the lake, the smaller tents clustered in a circle further back, the lines of the antenna hung bright with flagging, already a path worn to the garbage pit and the latrine. By the end of the summer this will seem like home, we will not want to admit the sadness we feel when we leave.

J.L. is on her knees stacking cans in neat rows on the shelves I've just finished building — tomatoes and peas and cream corn. It's the first time I've had a chance to talk to her.

"What do you do?" I ask. It seems a bad question, but I'm curious about her, why she would come up here.

She doesn't turn, but I can tell from her back and the tilt of her hat that she smiles.

"I cook."

I laugh. "I gathered that. I mean the rest of the time."

"Odds and ends," she says, pyramiding cans of apple juice. "I've been a cab driver, a waitress, a secretary. . . "

I drive another nail. "And?"

She stands up then and reaches in a long stretch, arms above her head. "I'm an arts student. Sociology, believe it or not."

I look at her quizzical, angular face. A scientist, I have always thought of arts students as slow and flabby, the men's voices pitched a shade high, the women infected with mannerisms. Katie is a dancer, but I always exclude her, her art is too physical, too disciplined. "You hardly seem the type."

"I'm not. It's a bunch of crap. Spend your whole life catering to people's problems. They wouldn't have any if nobody'd listen to them."

There's an untarnished brightness to her that reminds me of a new copper penny, as if she grabbed onto something and never let go, even if it wasn't always the right thing. I hope Jerome can't make her quit.

"What do you do?"

I start. "What do you mean? I'm a geologist."

She laughs. "Hell, how am I supposed to know? I thought everyone out here was a geologist, but Cap tells me he's an expediter and equipment man."

"In a camp this size you need someone like Cap to take care of logistics. He'll do some drafting, ship samples, stuff like that."

"Right now I'd think you were a carpenter. Is that table supposed to hold ten dancing bears?"

"Listen, I gotta build it right if it's going to last all summer. I built a table one summer that buckled right in the middle of the crew's favorite soup. Just sighed and leaned toward the end nobody was sitting at. There were only five of us, but I didn't take into account the elbows and the fist-poundings. Now I do."

"Will there be nine all summer?" She has her back to me, but for the first time I detect a hesitation on her part, as if she might have a pocket of fear that she's been trying to ignore. It hadn't occurred to me that she could be afraid, she seemed so tough in Yellowknife.

"Nine guys and you."

She says nothing.

"Hey, as long as you can cook you've got nothing to worry about. Guys in the bush don't think about anything but food."

"Great. And what about Jerome?"

"Ignore him."

She laughs bitterly. "That's always the solution. It's not so easy."

I look at her rigid back and then I get up and go outside into the whisper and ring of a settling camp. I feel the moss thick under my feet as I walk down to the gravel edge of the lake, where the two dozen brown bottles are already resting on the bottom, cooling in the green water. I fish out one, then turn, take two more and go back to the Jutland.

"Want a beer?" I hold out a bottle.

"Sure."

I open them with the Swiss army knife Katie gave me last

Christmas, toast J.L. before I drink. Then I take the third bottle, set it carefully on the crosspiece of the tent over the door. "One summer we had a cook that wouldn't drink, no matter what. He was an old guy, maybe sixty, couldn't tell where they dredged him up from. He wouldn't drink, but he had this full bottle of rye sitting above the door and he'd swear at it. 'You black-hearted bitch,' he'd say. 'You're not gonna get me, you mother-fucker, you goddamned whore.' He swore at that bottle all summer, but he never opened it, never had one drink. Then, the first night we were back in town I saw him in the bar and he was so plastered, I swear he couldn't even crawl. And I'll bet he spent the winter like that. So whenever you need something to swear at, there it is. You can pretend it's your worst enemy."

She laughs and takes a long swallow of beer, runs her hand along a shelf. "Hey, have you ever worked with Mackenzie before?"

"Sure have. Been partners for the last three summers."

She hesitates. "What's he like?"

"Best geologist in the company. Really knows his stuff. He found Meteor Ridge, you know."

"Meteor Ridge?"

"Yeah, big lead-zinc mine in B.C."

"Oh yes," she says doubtfully. She's obviously never heard of it. "He seems sad somehow. Does he have a family?"

Funny, I never thought of that. "I don't know. I suppose he does. There was some kind of gossip about him, but he's never said a word to me and I ignore the stories that go around. He's a good guy and I like him."

She's hanging pots and frying pans on hooks from the crossbar. I hammer one last nail into the table and she helps me to lift it upright. "There," I say. "Now I'll hook your stove up to the propane tank so you can make supper."

But before I let the tent flap fall shut behind me, I turn, point to the beer bottle squat and brown above me. "Don't forget, he was a good cook too."

Hearne

On the flight out I shoot film, poses of the tundra from Yellowknife west into the Yukon. The mountains there invite photographs. I get so carried away I have only three shots left when the pilot starts to bank and says, "There she is."

I take the first frame of the camp with my telephoto lens, otherwise the tents would be infinitesimal dots. But through the lens the white Jutland stands clearly; the orange tarps covering the six smaller tents are sharp triangles of color. Improbable, that fluorescent orange against the gray-green of the moss, the gray-blue of the mountains, the gray-white of the remaining snow.

The second is of the valley as the Twin Otter angles down to land on the lake. I hold my Nikon steady against the edge of the window, but even so the picture may come out blurred. Should make a note of that, jot it down before I forget. My slide logbook is new, crisp, the same kind of notebook I buy every summer to keep a record of my shots.

The third is of the assembled crew waiting as we motor slowly to the shore, floats half submerged from the weight of our load.

Jerome is the first one to jump ashore, already he's waving his arms and talking to Mackenzie while the rest of the crew forms a relay to unload the plane. I put my camera in the tin box to make sure it doesn't get wet before I edge along the float and jump. I've seen more things get dropped in a lake. Feels good to be on land after that stomach-jarring flight. Under the falling shadows of the mountains, the camp looks warm and busy. Tomorrow I'll get some rotten job because I wasn't here to help set up. Jerome insisted he needed two guys to load the fuel. Bastard never touched a drum himself, just climbed on board before we took off.

As for that Hudson, he's so terrorized he squeaks. Now he's standing there on shore gaping up at the mountains around the camp. Bet he's never seen one before. Trust Jerome to hire a Brit for an assistant, they're taking over geology. I'm glad Mackenzie's the party chief, maybe he'll let me get some wild helicopter shots.

Jerome

Those bastards start drinking before we get in. Mackenzie hasn't said a word, every one of 'em has three or four bottles stashed in their duffel bags. There's no way they're going to get any more, not if I have anything to say about it. Even the cook has got a beer bottle standing in the cooktent and when I ask her what it's doing there, she just laughs.

What a crew. The Jutland's set up facing the lake so the wind will hit that tent square every night. The Storm Havens aren't in a row, they're just any old way, one of those guys can easily sneak into the cook's tent. What they should have done is put her off by herself. And I suppose Thompson's already bunked in with Mackenzie. Well, he's getting thrown out. Mackenzie's not doing any office work without me knowing.

As for the rest of it. The garbage pit's too close and the shitter is too far away. Somebody's decided to build a shower. I've never been in a camp that needed a shower before, if you want to wash, you can wash in the lake. I suppose this is all for the cook's benefit. On top of that, the antennae are set up wrong. I know the radio won't work. And that damn Cap's set it up in his tent so that he won't have to get up in the morning for the sched, he can just lie in bed and talk to Mayo.

What a lazy bunch of bastards. They're all out here to make a lot of money and do as little as possible. Like Hearne, does nothing all day but take pictures. If you could get him to put the camera down long enough to pick up something else, it'd be a fucking miracle.

And Franklin, shit, he's always taking ten minutes off to do his "meditation." He wants to become a yogi or something. As for that kid Milton, he's so goddamn stupid he should have donkey's ears. Never been away from small-town Alberta before. Where in the hell did Mackenzie find these guys?

I can see that if anybody's going to find a mine this summer, it'll have to be me.

J.L.

I stand at the head of the long table that Thompson built this afternoon and I ladle, I spoon, I dish out steak and salad, vegetables and bread and butter, baked potatoes and sour cream. Thompson grins when he sees what I've made for this first supper.

"Meat and potatoes night, eh?"

"Thought I'd get off on the right foot," I say. "Besides, I haven't unpacked all my spices yet."

"I can hardly wait," he says. "Curry's my favorite."

Down the length of the table Jerome scowls but says nothing. He has moved in with Mackenzie and put Thompson with the helicopter pilot, so he feels guilty enough to restrain himself. And now they are all seated, two rows of masculine heads bent over melmac plates, silent except to reach for the salt, to clatter a knife on the oilcloth. I thought oilcloth didn't exist anymore, but there it was in the supplier's in Yellowknife, and of course I had to buy a length to cover the table.

They are so silent, absorbed while they eat, men are. Mackenzie looks at me and smiles, then returns to his plate. I can see the maps unrolling in his head, he's studying the contours of the mountains in the shape of the food he's eating. He's glad to be out here, away from town, the transition accomplished. This is his world, he moves effortlessly, the moss under his feet natural and yielding. The men obey him instinctively, Jerome blusters and shouts, but Mackenzie is in control as surely as he seems awkward and unassuming in town.

His world it is, and I have to halt, catch myself at the strangeness of this place. Where are we? The middle of a mountain range in the Yukon where I doubt any man has been before and, if so, left no trace, nothing behind. The mountains and the moss echo no residue of humans at all. And me, what am I doing here, a woman pretending to be a cook, pretending to have the nutritional welfare of these men foremost in my mind when all I wanted to find was silence, a relief from the cacophony of sound, of confession that surrounded, that always impinged on me. I didn't want their secrets, my ear not receptacle enough for ordinary words, let alone confession. I do not practice absolution.

Indeed, I have my own fear and my own doubt and my own confession to make, if there were anyone to listen. In the lengthening dusk I watch nine mouths chew and swallow, I watch nine pairs of eyes cover me and then look away. We are in the middle of the Yukon mountains with only tenuous radio contact to the outside world and I am on my own with or against them. At my own desire, at my own folly.

And quite suddenly I'm afraid. Me, self-contained but slight and alone and, yes, fearful, balanced against the anger and heft of nine men. With only the dubious position of cook to protect me.

I wanted this; I schemed to get here. And I think of walking across the uneven ground to my huddled tent, of lighting the Coleman lantern — but, no, every movement you make shows itself through the transparent tent walls. I may look like a boy, but I will have to undress in the dark every night.

And yet when I look at their faces down either side of this rough table, I see the same faces I have always seen, the same men I have always known. Bearded or clean-shaven, angular or smooth, they are after all only men. I have no reason to be afraid. I cannot be afraid or they will smell my fear, and I will certainly be lost, at their mercy. Keep them at bay with kettles, with pots and pans and wooden spoons, keep them on their knees with scalding water and merciless soups, keep them confused with the hieroglyphics only I can read in flour.

And now, searching for some source of strength, I think of Deborah, her bundle of faggots resting beside her as she reaches out a comforting hand. Deborah my friend, singer of joy and sorrow. We have more than once shored up our doubts and our losses together. Saving each other from ourselves, a woman's eternal lot.

She envied me coming here, retreating from the precast world. But when I told her it was easy, she smiled and shook her head. And of course she was right. It would be impossible for her, beautiful and soft and full of light, with that deep, broad voice. They would have no choice but to destroy her. It's easier for me, a girl shaped like a boy, with a boy's sharp angles.

Nine men. They are finishing now, shoving away their plates and scraping back their folding chairs and lighting cigarettes. I should have made a rule, no smoking in the cooktent. But it's too late now, and even though this is going to be my kitchen, it is already invaded.

Mackenzie clears his throat and looks at them, one by one. There have been few introductions. I hardly know their names. Now I can see he's going to say something, begin the summer officially, although we actually began it days ago, every one of us when we left wherever to come up north.

They are a miscellaneous lot, an odd assortment, not what I would have expected. I thought of geologists as solid, bearded men who smoked pipes and resembled one another. But as they turn to face him, expectant, I can see that they are hardly similar at all.

Mackenzie speaks without preamble, he cannot be pompous. "Well, I guess everything is pretty well set up. We have to finish building the shower, but Hearne, you and Cap can do that tomorrow."

"What do we need a shower for?" asks Jerome sourly. "The lake's full of water."

"That lake hasn't warmed up since the ice age," says Mackenzie. "Makes camp a lot more bearable if a guy can have a hot shower once in a while. They're easy enough to build. Other than that," and he looks at the men steadily, "breakfast is at seven, and you're all expected to be up by that time. After breakfast everyone will be given the day's work. Also, every day two of you will haul water for J.L. She's got enough to do cooking."

"Hey, I thought the cook hauled her own water," someone says.

"Not in this camp," says Mackenzie pleasantly. "Now, you've all been assigned a tent, it's up to you how you arrange that situation. If you really can't bear who you're bunking with, we'll try to arrange something. But I don't want to hear about any fighting. Oh, and by the way, those camp cots may seem uncomfortable, but get used to them. If you sleep on the ground you'll get rheumatism." He pauses, surveys them for a long moment as if their faces are maps. "We're supposed to be looking for uranium here. We'll be working on the claims the company's optioned and we may do some staking, if we find anything good. Questions?"

They shake their heads and I can see on their faces that desire to be out on the mountain, hammering boulders, walking the ridges. They all want to be the one who finds it, who discovers something, they will fight for that privilege.

And me, I clear the dirty dishes from the table, step around their feet and heat a pail of water to wash up with. There is something comforting in the familiar work, in my hands' movement from memory, an orchestration we women grow up with. Why does it seem that we're never taught how to do this, we simply know, we know the smoothest, most efficient way of making food and giving food and clearing up the remains of food, nourishers always. And perhaps why, when we are angry, we have a tendency to break, yes, dishes. Deborah once said that our lives are like the outer edge of china plates, sometimes smooth and sometimes scalloped, sometimes chipped, but always with an edge, always circular, ever-returning.

And me up to my elbows in soapy water scrubbing congealed food off melmac plates, rinsing them, stacking them in the remembered ceremony. By the end of the summer I will have washed more plates than I have in my entire life. I didn't count on that. I thought only of the making, the creating, the cooking. And discover I will spend more time washing dishes than I ever will cooking.

And before I can go outside and shut myself into my tent, I will make lunches, two dozen sandwiches buttered and sliced and wrapped, two dozen cookies and nine apples and all of them in brown bags lined up on the table waiting for the morning. Already I am tired. I only want to wrap myself in that down-filled sleeping bag and dream, dream lapped in the silence and the unhindered sweep of the moss and the mountains.

Mackenzie

And now, as the day fades behind me, I can finally let go. Above me the weave of the tent moves in a gyration of thread, belling to the wind that reaches under the rustle of the tarp. The camp is finally quiet, settled in the breath of sleep, under the overhang of the mountain. We're here. And it's good; I have almost forgotten the barrenlands in the rise and push of these mountains.

In the other cot Jerome stirs and snores softly, deaf to the keening whisper beyond the tent. Poor bastard. He misses all the best parts. And me, I miss a good companion. Jerome is next in command, so we're supposed to be together, but I wish I was sharing with Thompson. He too will be lying awake this first night, staring up into the darkness, hearing the mountain shift. And both of us lying like this, flat on our backs, we would talk softly, let the insufficient words fall between us. He is really too old to be my son, but he feels something like family to me. These last three summers together we've been excited by the same things, driven by the same urge. Yet he doesn't dig or pry, doesn't investigate my life. At least he's here and not on another project.

And now, J.L. Standing behind the table serving us steak and potatoes with that hat rammed on her head like it's her last defense. She even wears it when she eats. I wonder if she is asleep or if she too lies awake. I could go to her tent and ask her if she's all right, if she wants anything. But perhaps one of the men is already there, wangled his way into acting as comfort. Of course, it's none of my business. I'm afraid that if I did go to her, she'd think that's what I wanted, to crawl into her sleeping bag. I wonder if she'll stay, if she can last out the summer.

Lying in a tent in the darkness one is enclosed in febrility, the sharp sense that outside the wind sweeps unhindered, there is no light, no movement, perhaps even no world. And as I feel my body emptying itself, flowing into the shape of the cot under my sleeping bag, I know I will find again the sharp and spiny edge that the city has dulled with dust and grit, that has been worn down by fluorescent lights and routine and the plastic edges of office furniture.

Even if there is nothing here, and it doesn't look good — that claim group has mineralization, but it's mostly isolated in a few breccia pipes — we're here. Tomorrow the helicopter will drop me on a ridge and I can walk, move from outcrop to outcrop, draw the contours on my map, feel the grain of the rock in my hand, the straps of my pack against my shoulders.

And just before my eyes close over sleep, I feel again a brush along my skin, a caress down my side, the same sensation when Janice moved toward me, the way her hands would lock themselves around the small of my back to hold me deep inside her.

We're here.

Milton

I figured you could get closer to God up here, but He feels farther away. That girl. I better not forget to read my Bible.

If they could plant wheat or run cattle on these mountains, a man could get rich. I suppose it's too bare, only good for growing rock and how would you ever get them up here? But if I save up my money, maybe I can buy a quarter section in Peace River country. A real homestead. Some of our church went there. They say it's hard work, but you can buy land without a bank loan.

J.L.

And after they fall asleep, I lie awake beside them in the dark, holding myself perfectly still so that I will not disturb them. Beside me the weight in the bed is a tension, something I want to move away from. They breathe quietly in sleep, present in the palpable darkness, but distant, so far removed they might just as well not be there. They turn and rustle, I feel the abrasion of another skin, a heavy leg thrown across mine. Present they are, yet absent from me, only another body in the other half of the bed, it hardly matters who. I never think of them, only of myself lying awake, staring wide-eyed and sleepless. And if they moan and stir I reach out a hand, slide it over the turn of a muscle to reassure them.

Lying there, I make notes, evaluate, dream, rid myself of their words. Piecing, stitching seams that threaten to come loose, soaking up the emanation of another body. Sponge, a woman is a sponge. We can be infinitely compressed, infinitely engorged, and still spring back to our own shape. And all for them, all at their whim and mercy, the inert weight on the other side of the bed. Even so, I take a comfort in the deep regularity of their breathing, in their thick and jointed bodies.

Their inappropriateness never fails to amaze me. They discriminate so little over where and when. To be so much controlled by hormones, excretions. Perhaps if they would learn to start at the beginning it would be easier, they would be able to push me further. But individually, collectively, they assume that I am ready, primed, they behave as if there has been another man immediately before, preparing my anticipation and response. Still, I turn to them, I seek them out, I wait for the perfect lover. There is comfort in another body in the bed.

And now, here I am. They weighed me up and down at supper. Even if I do look like a boy I could see them calculating how long it will take before they dare to rasp the zipper on my tent, before they can make some excuse to stumble over my guy ropes. But this summer is mine. I'll keep my hat on my head, I'll keep my hands away from belt buckles, I'll listen but I won't hear. It would be a shame to spoil the silence.

I turn on my side, close my eyes against the darkness. And then, under me, I feel the flank of the mountain shift, feel it rumble and groan as if settling the camp in its arms. And I open mine, arch my body in anticipation, waiting. But it is only a greeting; the rumble subsides and the last thing I remember is the musty smell of the sleeping bag against my nose.

Hudson

Where in colonial hell are we? I couldn't find my way out of here if I tried. They're mad, every one of them, mad. And me, I'm fixed with that bloody Jerome all summer. He shouts at me like I'm a stray dog. Hudson, do this! Hudson, come here! Hudson, fetch that! It's not exactly what I came over here to study geology for.

And these mountains. Bare, gray, no trees, no grass. They surround you, they press you down, they laugh at you like teeth. It's almost June and they are still snow-covered. I'm sure nobody knows where we are.

Besides that, I get stuck in a tent with this weird religious kid. He comes off a farm somewhere, came up here to make money. Before he goes to bed he lies down on the floor of the tent and starts to do a complicated series of leg and shoulder exercises. I'm so damn tired I can hardly get my clothes off. "What are you doing?" I ask. Maybe he thinks exercising will work out the kinks.

All he says is, "The body is the temple of the spirit," and starts to do pushups. When he's done about fifty, he sits on the edge of his cot and opens a Bible. Then he hauls out an exercise book and jots notes in it with a smeary pencil stub while he reads.

I have to say something. "Hey, do you take this religious stuff seriously?"

He raises his head and stares at me as if the question is utterly preposterous. "It is the true word."

I shake my head. "You're not going to keep doing that in this camp. Did you see those mountains? By the end of the day we'll be so tired we won't be able to stand up."

"They are an example of God's glory."

"God's glory. They look murderous to me."

"Would you like to pray with me?" he says. "It will make you feel better."

Hastily I crawl inside my sleeping bag. Why did I get stuck with this nut? "Not tonight, thanks," I say to the wall of the tent. "I'm hardly a great believer in the efficacy of prayer."

But I can't restrain my curiosity and I roll over to look at him. Damn if he isn't kneeling on the ground with his hands folded and propped on the cot in front of him. His bent head murmurs softly, and the back of his neck is scrubbed red under the edge of his dark and curly hair. "If you're praying anyway," I say, "maybe you could throw in a request to get that bloody Jerome off my back."

He nods and keeps murmuring.

But when the Coleman lantern has hissed out and he is rustling into his sleeping bag, I suddenly want to talk to him, the silence of those mountains outside is so heavy. "What religion are you?"

"Mennonite," he says.

"Mennonite? What's that?"

"Christian."

"Protestant?"

"Yes. Anabaptist."

"Never heard of it before."

"Not many people have," he says, and it is the first time he speaks without that country inflection, that intonation and cadence of words that even compared to Canadian English is slangy and slurred, the mark of a distinct and isolated community. You'll find it sometimes up in Yorkshire, pockets of people whose speech is so inbred that the pronunciation grates the ears.

God, I wish I was home. I should have taken Papa's offer, the airfare home and the summer at Bath. Instead, I decide I want to be adventurous and see some real geology in the Canadian north. Mad. There's nothing here for anyone. We're in the middle of the bloody wilderness and we could just as easily never get out again.

And if I have to be Jerome's assistant, I won't learn a thing about geology. I'll be nothing more than a batboy. I could as well have stayed in Edmonton and read my textbooks for next year.

Cap

Women.

When we got down to the dock with all the gear, I figured she was just one of those Yellowknife hippies sitting there. Even when we started loading the stuff and she pitched in, I didn't think nothing of it. Lots of chicks around looking for something to do, talk to the pilots, get a ride sometimes. But when Mackenzie arrives with the last truckload, and he acts like she's coming along, it dawns on me that she's our cook. I thought that game in the bar was a joke! And now here we are, with a genuine female cook! Mackenzie just acts like it's perfectly normal.

In the plane she sits beside me and when we've lifted off, she turns, grinning a little. "What's the matter?"

"I'm embarrassed. Didn't know you were the cook."

She laughs. "I'm getting used to that reaction."

"Guess we'll be seeing a lot of each other then."

She looks puzzled. "Guess so."

"I mean, in camp. I'm the expediter, radio operator, camp logistics, odds-and-ends man. Capital Kane is my name."

"You're not a geologist?"

"Hell no, never could stand the thought of going to university for four years just to learn a lot of complicated words."

"You take care of the radio?"

"Right. Communications officer. General campman. That's why we'll be seeing a lot of each other. I ship samples, do some drafting, fix stuff. Need a guy like me in a camp this size. You've got a job, cooking for nine men!"

"I thought I was going to be alone all day," she says.

I laugh. "Don't worry, I'll be around to protect you from the bears."

Funny, she looks disappointed. I know I'm no ladykiller, but I'm a nice guy, women learn to like me. I have to smile to myself. Goddamn Mackenzie, after all these years, up and hires a female cook. He could have picked a better-looking one, but shit, a girl is a girl. I ain't complaining.

And she seems amiable enough, jokes and talks with everybody. We split open a case of beer on the way up. Good thing we got the plane with Mackenzie. Jerome wouldn't let us drink, too damn scared we'd all be drunk by the time we got there. But Mackenzie's easy, has a beer himself, even though he's hunched over, concentrating on his map. Hell knows where we'll end up. Guess our closest contact will be Mayo. I'll have to set up a radio sched and arrange for an expediter there as quick as I can. Just hope the goddamn antenna gets here in one piece.

Shit, a whole summer in camp with a female cook. Hard to believe.

Thompson

After we've breakfasted on platters of pancakes and fried eggs, Mackenzie sits and picks his teeth for a long thoughtful moment. Finally he looks at me and says, "Where's the rifle, Thompson?"

"It's in our tent," says Jerome. "Can't leave that damn thing lying around."

"Go put a round in it and bring it here — okay, Thompson?"

"What the hell do you intend to do?" says Jerome. "We got no time for target practice now, we got to get out there on that mountain."

"The mountain isn't going anywhere. Small matter should be taken care of first."

J.L. is washing dishes, but I can sense that her back stiffens. I go off to get the gun and Jerome follows me. In their tent I pick up the rifle — a 303 Enfield — and fit some shells into the chamber.

"Hell, if we're gonna play around with guns," says Jerome, and what does he haul out of his duffel bag but the meanest-looking handgun I've ever seen, a 44 Magnum. I thought they were illegal for common citizens.

"Where did you get that?"

He smirks. "Police. Have to have a special license, special training. Can't allow everybody to carry one of these."

"You're crazy. What in hell do you need a thing like that for?"

He grins, shrugs. "You never know."

The guy is a maniac. No wonder his wife looks like a scared rabbit. I hope he doesn't get bushed. I've never worked with him before.

In the cooktent, Mackenzie hefts the rifle, then says quietly to J.L., "You got a minute?"

She turns, drying her hands on a checkered dishtowel. "What?"

"Come on outside."

She stands, rubbing her hands on the towel, then flings it over the back of a chair, shoves back her hat and slowly follows him.

Jerome appears around the corner of the tent. "You're not going to teach *her* to shoot?"

Mackenzie just looks at him.

"She doesn't need to know how to shoot. Cap is in camp all the time!"

Mackenzie lifts the rifle to his shoulder and sights through it. "Everybody learns how to shoot. What happens if a bear starts mauling Cap?"

Jerome sneers. "Pretty unlikely."

Mackenzie tears a piece of cardboard from one of the boxes waiting to be burned. He draws a large face on it with his felt pen, blacks in a nose, eyes, a mouth, then hands it to me and points away from the camp. "Go stick this up over there."

J.L. clears her throat. "Uh, Mackenzie, I don't think this is really necessary."

"J.L.," he says, "in my camp everybody knows how to shoot a gun. Same rules apply to you."

I stick the cardboard face up on a stake and come back to find him showing her how to hold the rifle while Jerome stands there with a scornful look.

"Ever shot one of these before?"

She shakes her head. I can see that she doesn't like it.

"Well, it's not hard at all, but a gun is only as good as the person handling it. You have to respect it. Now, hold the stock tight against your shoulder because when you fire, it will kick. Slide the bolt back and ram it forward like this. That cocks the gun. Line up your sights there, then just squeeze the trigger."

She has never touched a gun before, I can tell. It is not

only heavy and awkward for her but it fills her with distaste. And by now the whole damn camp is standing silently behind me, watching her, Hearne clicking his relentless camera.

"Take off that hat," says Mackenzie. He swipes it off her head and throws it on the ground behind her. "Okay, don't let it point up or down, just hold it steady. Practice now. Aim at the target and squeeze the trigger. It's on safety, so nothing will happen."

Carefully, her face set, she does everything exactly the way he's told her.

"All right," he says, "you got the idea." She lets the gun point to the ground.

"Don't point the gun at your feet. Even if it's on safety, it's dangerous, you'll blow your toes off," says Mackenzie.

"It's so heavy."

"Try it again. Is it starting to feel more familiar?"

She nods, brings the stock back to her shoulder, squints into the sights, then squeezes.

"Don't hold it too loosely. It'll kick like hell."

"Let's see her shoot it," says Jerome. He's toying with the Magnum, as if he wants to try himself.

Mackenzie glances at him but says nothing, his attention on J.L. "Want to try it for real?"

"Do I have to? I think I could shoot in an emergency."

"Yes, you have to." He clicks off the safety. "Okay, remember, hold it steady and aim at the target." He is so completely patient that I think, irrelevantly, what a good father he must be.

J.L. shifts her feet and points the gun. For a long moment she rests her finger on the trigger, then begins to tighten it. I can see that she's not holding the stock firmly against her shoulder, but Mackenzie says nothing. Suddenly, the gun explodes with a crash. The bullet raises a puff of dust far to the right of the target and J.L. is sprawled flat on her back on the ground.

Jerome is the one who laughs aloud, who sets off the

quieter snickers of the crew until they're all roaring.

Mackenzie does not laugh. He picks up the gun and helps her to her feet, ignoring everyone. "Kick like a mule. You've got to hold the stock tight against your shoulder. Just watch me."

The crew is clowning and making rude remarks. J.L.'s face is dead white and absolutely set, her body strung so tight with humiliation that I want to grab the gun out of Mackenzie's hands and shout, "Leave her alone. Why should she have to learn to shoot the fucking thing?" But of course I don't. You have to stick to the rules and the party chief makes them. Instead, I turn around and scowl at the men. "Shut up, you assholes." It doesn't help.

Mackenzie cocks the rifle, takes aim and fires at the target. Again that crash and the echo from the mountains.

"Let's see if you hit it," says Jerome, and jogs over to the target. "Got an eye," he shouts, "but you missed the nose." He comes running back. "Let me show you how to do it."

Mackenzie just looks at him. "Get yourself a belt holster for that gun," he says. "You can't carry it loose."

I can't tell if Jerome even heard him, he's so busy sighting over the blue barrel of that deadly Magnum. He loves it. You can tell by the way he holds it, legs apart and arms extended, police stance and all, with the whole crew standing there watching. The bastard loves it, he's a goddamn show-off.

Then, *whamm!* "I hit it dead on. I know I did!" he yells.

I run over to the target with him. There is a second bullet hole just below the mouth. "Off-center," I say.

"Shit," he says sourly. "The sun was in my eyes."

We walk back to the group, a half-circle of men standing around a gun. "Let me try it again," says J.L. quietly. There is instant silence. Nine pairs of eyes watch her as she lifts the rifle to her shoulder, slides the bolt back and rams it forward, sights carefully and then, perfectly calm and steady, tightens her finger on the trigger.

I almost close my eyes. Let her hit it, at least let her hit it, I think.

Crash. The mountains repeat the sound back and forth between themselves. Jerome and I both run to the cardboard target, Jerome open-mouthed and for once speechless in front of the perfect hole dead through the center of that round black nose.

"Bull's-eye!" I yell, but when I turn to see her triumph, she has already handed the gun back to Mackenzie and, ignoring the astonished crew, dusts off her hat and walks to the cooktent to finish washing the breakfast dishes.

Mackenzie

A. Check claim locations

B. Map geology

C. Grid survey — Analytical work

D. Radiometric survey

E. Reconnaissance work

Analytical Plans:

1. Stream Sediment Sampling

2. Water Sampling

3. Soil Sampling

4. Outcrop Sampling

Sample Treatment Procedure

I. *Hand Samples*

1. Description of texture, homogeneity, mineralogy, alteration, veining

2. Radioactivity

3. Fluorescence

4. Bagging/Filling Sample shipping advice forms

5. Rock Geochemistry — lab analysis

6. Geochemistry results interpretations

II. *Soil/Silt Samples*

1. Description of particle size

2. Soil color

3. pH

4. Radioactivity

5. Sample bagging/Shipping forms

6. Uranium Fluorometric analysis in Lab

7. Atomic Absorption analysis in Lab

8. Interpretation of Results

Roy

I'm the pilot that flies them fuel, food and mail once a week. Wednesdays. It's a long flight from Mayo, but I don't mind, it's beautiful country. They can hear me long before I get there. When my floats touch water they are standing on the shore of the lake, waiting. She said to me once, "You're our only contact with the outside world." And grinned at me, showing a perfect line of small teeth. As if it was a joke.

It's a strange camp. It has an air of careful control, as if things are never out of place and if they are, ignored into line. There's tension, but it's not the same tension that you find in most camps. All-male camps are full of restrained madness, furious work. And usually camps that have a woman are full of joking, nudges, sex. If there's a woman, they're screwing at least one of the guys. But that's not happening here, I can tell. It's almost as if they're afraid of her. I can't see that it's her fault, she doesn't seem bitchy to me. It's more than that, she's done something to them so that they're not quite sure of her, they keep their distance. Yet they like her, everybody's always joking around.

Hell, I can't figure it. Maybe it has something to do with Mackenzie, he's an old bush hand. Hard to tell about him too, just a quiet, reasonable guy. Only saw him once since I flew them in. When I come, he's usually out on traverse, works harder than the rest of the crew does. It's always her and Cap, and sometimes the helicopter pilot is there. Last week I got there late in the afternoon and the crew was straggling in while we unloaded. They've got equipment for a radiometric survey, must be looking for uranium.

One of them comes over and starts hauling into me about bringing the crew liquor, says it's my responsibility to make sure the expediter doesn't slip booze in with the supplies. I just laugh and tell him I'm no prohibition board. It's the party chief that makes the rules about booze or no booze and Mackenzie doesn't mind.

Well, this guy tirades at me like it's my fault that the crew doesn't work harder. I tell him to go fuck himself and just for emphasis the cook comes out with a twenty-dollar bill and asks if I'd bring a bottle of good scotch next week, that Mackenzie wants it. That bastard gets really red, but he shuts up, just glowers at the cook like he'd be happy to murder her.

So I had a private little laugh.

Still, she's a queer one. Not much to her, you'd hardly notice her if she wasn't the only woman around. And not exactly what you'd call attractive, hardly a curve on her. Even so, a woman is a woman, and when you're in the middle of nowhere, you can't afford to be picky. So what's with those guys? She doesn't seem to be saving herself for a guy back home either, that's not the reason. The only letters she sends are to some woman called Deborah. I take their mail out, and I've looked.

Well, something is bound to happen by the end of the summer. We're all human.

Franklin

A candle clear to fix my thoughts upon.

There we are, slogging up and down the mountains every day, sorting rock samples and soil samples every night, keeping our field notes, adding details to the big map. And what does she think of us?

I've started a sequence of poems about her, about the way she cooks, about the way she washes dishes with her hat on, about the way she looks straight through us and beyond.

She is mysterious, she tells us nothing about herself. Why is she up here? I've asked her and she only laughs and shrugs, turns away from me. Sometimes she seems black and tense, as if she has some deep and far-away worry. I try to talk to her about meditation, but she only snorts and says she has no use for it, she doesn't want to suspend thinking. Still, even her contempt is fascinating.

It's when I'm up on the mountain that I can meditate best, that I can find words for the poems. High as the eagles, that's when I know my soul is purest. I'm glad we were sent here, it's better than the tundra for my karma. I like geology but I'd rather be a poet or a philosopher. Geology is a way to seek out the wilderness.

I could make her understand if she would let go of her disbelief for only a few minutes. But she's bitter, tight and bitter. The one chance I got to tell her about her aura, about the way meditation enables you to see beyond a person's outer shell into their soul, she laughed a small, disagreeable laugh.

"You're a romantic," she says. "That won't solve any problems."

"If every man knew himself, the world's problems would be eliminated."

For once she looks straight at me, and her lips are twisted a little. Then she turns away and her voice is brittle and unbending. "That's an excuse. People know themselves, they simply aren't interested in changing."

And oh, how bright she burns.

Milton

She can cook. She's not the way a girl should be, but she can cook. We're eating homemade bread and banana loaf, salads and soups and dishes I never heard of. She even makes oatmeal with raisins in the morning.

I never seen a girl like her before. She is hard and angry-like instead of soft and still and holding inside the way a girl should be. The girls in church, you can hardly see them moving under their wide cotton skirts. If you touched them, they would feel like feather pillows. It's wrong to think of that — feeling. But she does it, makes me think, I can't help it, she is all elbows and corners and even her hair is not long and smooth the way a girl's should be, but short and spiky, like a chewed-up cat's.

Our elders would say that she is lost. But she can cook.

Mackenzie

My first traverse is an angle across the claim group to look at the original showing and to determine the extent of the mineralization. The prospector's map is optimistic, he thinks there is stratiform uranium, but all I can find are small veins here and there in the intrusive rocks. P.Q. has bought a line, but what can you expect, a uranium prospect is a difficult thing to assess. Still, we'll run the radiometric survey. We might find more than I think.

Even so, it feels tremendously good to be out again. When the noise of the Jet Ranger finally dies away, I stand for a moment looking at the plunge of the valley. It's been a while since I worked in the Yukon, I'd forgotten how it gets hold of you. From here, high on the lean slopes of the mountains, the summer looks better already. I open my jacket and stretch out my arms, let the wind bell it around me. A man could rest here, could press himself into the moss and let the mountain grow around him.

And even the camp is better than I expected. The crew has such a dislike for Jerome that he can't undermine me, already they are cracking silent jokes about him. I'll just have to keep him busy. One thing is sure — he works hard. But he over-reacts to everything. I don't know if I dare to go out and leave him in charge. If I do there might be carnage, when I get back the camp will probably be smoking.

I usually go out for a week, the one holiday I take. Go out and get in the Ford and drive, drive around the city, drive around the province, look for them. Someday I'll see them, the three of them having a picnic on the beach or in a park, Janice with her pale face turned up to catch the sun, ignoring the kids who will be running, playing tag, pelting each other. I wait for that moment, watch for them, know that someday I will see them, I will find them, I will have one perfect chance to explain to them and everything will be resolved.

But I forget. Sandy is seventeen; Stevie is fifteen. They won't be playing tag. And suddenly, standing with the wind trying to push me off the mountain, I realize that I won't go out this summer, I'll stay here. I won't look for them anymore because even if I find them, how will I know it's them? And how can I explain something I don't understand myself?

God. I huddle down beside a boulder, put my hand on its surface to steady myself. All these years and I don't understand it myself.

Hold on, hold on Mackenzie, you're getting soft, the mountains have jinxed you, why are you thinking of *them* on the first day you're out on traverse? Look, look, down there on the valley is a huddle of tents, you're up here to find a mine. Down there is a crew and a cook and somewhere up here is a mine. You just have to find it.

J.L. Incredible, this morning, that look on her face. I thought she'd turn around and pick off the whole crew one by one, cool as you please. Instead, she blasts smack through the middle of the target.

And me, I have to keep a poker face, can't show any pleasure or they'll all start to hate her. She has to do it on her own. Still, it was something, that set to her jaw, her eyes narrowed into slits, the force of her anger so strong I thought she would evoke the whole mountain down on us. Christ, what a beginning.

Beginning. Come on, Mackenzie, sling that pack on your back and take a reading on your compass and start walking. The crew is checking the claim locations and you're supposed to map the original showing. Walk, Mackenzie, walk.

Cap

"Break, break, this is LG twenty-four calling Mayo twelve. LG twenty-four calling Mayo twelve. Do you read me, over?"

"LG twenty-four, this is Mayo twelve. We copy, over."

"Do you think you can send the plane in a day early? We're running low on helicopter fuel, over."

"We can try, but I'll have to check if he's booked that day, over."

"Good. You got last week's grocery list from the pilot, over?"

"That's affirmative, over."

"Add ten pounds of flour. And a carton of cigarettes too, over."

"Can do. Looks like you got good cooking up there, over."

"Good cooking but that's it, over."

"Too bad. You guys must be doing something wrong, over."

"Just you worry about yourself, Mayo. Talk to you tomorrow at six, over."

"Right on, Cap. Anything else, over?"

"Nope. Over and out." I put the mike on the hook and lie back on the cot again. It was a great idea to install the radio right here beside my bed. I don't even have to get up in the morning. Except when everyone comes crowding in to hear what's happening in Mayo. These damn six o'clock radio scheds. Maybe I can get them to slot us for seven, get an extra hour of shut-eye.

Jeez, the whole Yukon knows about her already. Hard to believe.

J.L.

In that one frozen moment, lying flat on my back on the ground with the wind hammered out of me, I almost lose control. I almost jump up and cock that gun and turn it on them, Jerome first. And I wouldn't have missed. If it wasn't for Mackenzie I would have, I would have gladly killed them all. But he didn't laugh, he didn't even crack a smile, he just ignored them and picked me up and oh so patiently showed me how to do it again.

And Jerome showing off with that ridiculous Magnum. It made me realize my own power, that I could turn a gun on them and pull the trigger, that up here there are no rules, no set responses, everything is new and undefined, we are beyond, outside of the rest of the world. There are no controls here.

It frightens me and yet I know now that I don't have to be afraid of them, no not afraid at all. Out here my anger is as real as theirs, can have as great an effect. And that's when I can take the rifle again, take it and hold it tight and hard against my shoulder, the polished stock under my hand. I slam back the bolt and then thrust it forward, balance myself on the balls of my feet, sight. Far down the barrel I see the black nose on that cardboard face. Without moving, without taking my eyes away, I touch my finger to the trigger, cold and smooth, and squeeze. *Crash*. The mountains resound angrily.

I give the gun to Mackenzie and walk away. I know I've hit it. I know they won't forget.

Thompson

I've known him for long enough to guess that something happened to him that first day. When the chopper brought him back he dumped fifty pounds of rocks out on the plywood floor of the cooktent, then started looking at them with his hand lens, one by one, on his knees. It looks like he's practically taken a sample grid of the claim area all by himself. J.L. is cooking something tomato spicy that I could smell all the way up the mountain. She ignores Mackenzie, just stands there chopping celery with a white towel tied over her jeans and that hat on her head.

"Go get Cap," he says to me when I come in.

Cap is hammering a tarp around the woodframe shower stall. When he sees the pile of rocks on the floor he whistles. "Hey, Mackenzie, you want to ship the whole mountain back home in one day?"

"There's the list," he says. "You label them and get them ready to send out. I want them on the next plane for assay. There'll be more tomorrow."

Just then Jerome pushes into the tent. "Jesus," he says, "didn't you do any mapping?"

Mackenzie just looks at him and I know he's not only described every one of those samples in detail, but he's been mapping too.

He turns to Cap again. "Oh, and ask them to assay for copper and silver and gold. That way we might find something."

I've never seen him so upset. He doesn't take it out on us, but he pushes himself, works harder than ever. And that's something, because he always works harder than the rest of the crew anyway. He believes that the party chief has to set an example. It's like he's trying to sweat something out of his system, but damn if I can figure out what might have hit him up there on the mountain.

Maybe he's starting to feel his age. He's one of the oldest geologists that still goes out in the field every year. And it must be a pressure, the long summer stretching in front of us. Still, he shouldn't quit, he's the best there is. I can't see him as an office geologist, formations and contours nothing more than the lines and colors on maps.

There's that sadness in him that I've always felt, but never wanted to ask about. We're friends but it's none of my business. He leaves me alone too. But damn if it doesn't make me worry. I've never seen him like this, so heavy and black.

And it makes me wonder what will happen to me, will these mountains get into my system the way they've gotten into his. I try to explain it to Katie: that it's another part of my life, that it's separate, different, but even though I know she tries, she doesn't see what it means to me. She doesn't mind my going away. I think she likes it because she can work harder, but then I get scared because I don't want to trade her for the mountains or the barrenlands either.

I still can't believe that I found her, can hardly believe that someone like her exists. She is quicksilver, moving, always moving, she is herself a dance. I keep wanting to tell J.L. about her, to ask if the feeling is real, will it last, am I doing the right things? It's silly, she doesn't even know Katie, but I have a feeling she would understand.

But Mackenzie makes me worry. Every day he pulls a pack full of rocks that nobody could carry out of the helicopter, fifty sometimes sixty pounds. As if the sheer weight of the rocks on his back will keep him upright. Good thing we've got the helicopter to drop us off and pick us up. If we were in a camp without one, he'd kill himself. How can I say anything to him, we're friends. And for the first time in all the years I've known him, I don't want to be like him when I get to be his age.

Mackenzie

What did she really want? I never asked her, but even if I had, would she have told me? It's been eating at me now for weeks, I can hardly think of anything else. This property isn't any good, there's not enough uranium here to power a firecracker, we're wasting our time, and over and over again I keep thinking that I never knew, I never knew.

What did she want? All these years trying to find her, waiting for her to come back, and it never occurred to me to ask, the idea of it never even occurred to me before. I can only think it through, somewhere I'll discover an answer.

I come home on Thursday night, the middle of the week, we're going camping on the weekend. The house is strangely silent, there's no supper cooking, no children's noise, the television is blank. Janice has taken them shopping, didn't allow for the traffic. I find a package of hamburger and begin the sauce for spaghetti. I like cooking when Janice isn't around to watch me make mistakes. She's so much more efficient, but it's restful to work in the kitchen. Chop onions and brown the meat, stir in tomatoes and garlic, add oregano, basil and a bay leaf. Turn it down and leave it to simmer while I put the spaghetti on.

This year I'll be doing exploration in the Northwest Territories, working up around the Arctic Islands. Proposals have all been made and pretty soon the projects will be assigned. It looks like I'll get what I want. Finding Meteor Ridge last year puts me in a pretty good position. They're pleased with that. Exploration hasn't found much lately. A promotion, more money, maybe we'll even move to a better house.

I'll have a scotch while I'm waiting. I have to watch that, scotch sneaks up on you over the years. In the living room I flick on the television and watch the news, still thinking about my project. Proposal time always tires me out, the pressure, the waiting.

At eight I wake up to the smell of burnt tomatoes and artificial laughter from the television. Upstairs Sandy and Steve's rooms are quiet, orderly, toys put away. I'm suddenly afraid to go into ours. But when I push open the door, it too is neat, the wide bed made as smooth and tight as always, the closet doors closed, the damp towel picked up from where I flung it this morning.

Frantically I pull open the closet. Her clothes hang in a neat row, party dresses covered in plastic, summer and winter clothes neatly divided. Wait, her red sweater, the bright wool sweater that she loves so much. I rifle through the hangers, remember seeing it this morning when I pulled out a clean shirt. And it's gone, the only thing she took.

Hold it, Mackenzie, hold it. I go downstairs to the garage. She's taken the Volkswagen. Something must have happened — a flat tire, an accident. And even while I phone the police, I know I'm only postponing realization. No, nobody by that name has reported an accident, if something happened I would be informed. Missing persons? They must be gone for at least forty-eight hours to be considered missing. Don't panic, sir, they're sure to turn up.

She sends the note to the office, postmarked Thursday. "Dear Earl, we're all right. I'm sorry. I hope you'll understand. Janice." Understand what? I don't understand, goddamn it. She'll come back, I know she will. I just have to wait long enough and she'll come to her senses.

Ten years ago and I still don't understand, I still don't know what got into her.

Janice. That cherry-red sweater and the way you wouldn't sleep the night before I left for the field. I'd wake up and you would be huddled against me, shivering. It happened every summer. I don't feel guilty about that. I told you before we got married that I was a geologist, I had to go out in the field every year, and if you weren't prepared for that we shouldn't get married. I didn't lie to you, you knew what to expect.

Somehow I know it wasn't my absence, it was something else. But what? And why didn't you tell me, give me a chance to change it? I cared. I would have tried to do something. I may have been stupid but I didn't want you to be unhappy, I would have let you do anything you wanted. I just couldn't read your mind.

So what did you really want? Was it so impossible that I couldn't give it to you, was it so impossible to ask me? I would have done anything. I would still do anything to make you come back, even if I'd hardly know you now.

And what did I do wrong? I didn't hit you once. I never played around. I never complained about you spending money, I liked it when you bought something for yourself instead of always for the children, for the house, for the yard. I know I was moody and preoccupied, I know I was messy, I know I'd fall asleep after supper instead of talking to you, but is that what made you leave?

I still don't know. I'll wake up at four o'clock tonight and stare at the early light filtering through the green tent and I'll go over the list again, thinking that I've forgotten something important, or that I'll suddenly understand. Jerome will snore happily, he never worries about his wife, says he doesn't think about her up here, doesn't even write her a letter once in a while.

If I could find something up here, I could sleep, I could forget about her. If I can only find a mine.

Ivan

Every morning I go out and start her up, rev the motor until the blades begin to whine. Jet Rangers are good machines. They're ready to go quick. By that time Mackenzie has given his orders and I take the first crew out. I can only carry four men, so I make two trips. Takes an hour or so. Depends on how far they go.

Once I drop everybody off I just have to wait until it's time to pick them up again. Sometimes Mackenzie wants to be moved in the middle of the day, but otherwise I take it easy. I spend a lot of time in the chopper reading *Playboy*, waiting. Always arrive at the spot where I'm supposed to pick them up a little early. Keeps everybody happy, especially if it's cold and rainy. The rest of the time I work on the machine. Make sure everything is in good shape, avoid the problems before they happen. The biggest problem is keeping track of the crew when the chopper is running and they're liable to lose their heads in a blade.

Even when I'm in camp I don't have much to do with her. The coffee's always on the stove and she's always cheerful, but she doesn't exactly invite company. Some afternoons we have a game of poker. She always wins. Never met a girl that was such a cool gambler. And something is always simmering or stewing or boiling on her stove. I can't figure how she cooks some of those things. It's just a dinky little propane job. Four burners, sure, but it's the size of a doll's stove. I don't know how she bakes bread in that oven.

Cap usually stays in camp. He is always hanging around, sniffing, scratching himself, acting like general nuisance. I can see he's trying to put the hustle on her, but he doesn't seem to be getting anywhere. She ignores him. Steps around his feet as if he isn't there. Goes on rolling out pie crust or chopping vegetables for soup. He's not a great talker. I guess he figures that just sitting there and looking at her is going to get him somewhere.

Sometimes if it's nice she vanishes for an afternoon. Like she needs to be alone. Once, flying out to pick up the early crew, I saw her far up the valley toward the base of the mountain. She was stooped over, looking at the ground. Then she straightened up and put something in a little bag. Queer. Must have been collecting rocks.

She's got to be the queerest girl I ever met in my life. We've been out here a couple of weeks now and I don't know her any better than I did at first. Even if I do see her every day. And I have a feeling that by the end of the summer I still won't. She doesn't talk much. Sometimes she cracks a crazy joke. She'll take a drink, but at night she goes to bed early. Doesn't like to hang around the cooktent with the men. Since she has to be up at six, I guess I can't blame her.

Still, a person seems to want to talk to her. Maybe because it's like she doesn't listen. Does what she's doing and pays no attention, every once in a while just shoves her hat back. Funny thing, at the beginning of the summer I thought she looked like a boy. Now she seems more female than most women I remember. Being out here changes your ideas some.

One sunny morning I'm sitting in the chopper waiting for Mackenzie and Thompson so that I can drop them off in the next valley. I've already taken the rest of the crew out. They're on the base line doing a grid with the scintillometer. Jerome supervising, of course. Through the bubble I see her beside the cooktent, dishtowel in hand. Watching the helicopter like she thinks it's some strange bird. Standing there, she reminds me of a disappointed little kid. So when Mackenzie gets into the seat beside me, I say, "Hey, anything wrong with giving J.L. a ride?"

He looks surprised. "Of course not. Hasn't she ever ridden in this thing?"

"No. I don't think she has."

"Well sure." He gets out, head down, runs to where she's

standing and says something to her.

Her face lights up. She throws that dishtowel over one of the tent's guy ropes. Grabs her hat with one hand and scrambles in beside Thompson. They both grin at each other. Then we're away. The chopper lifts off the ground with that quick, satisfying turn, the sheer, air-defying will of it. Some pilots call these machines egg beaters. I call it my flying carpet.

We rise and swing out for a lower point to cross the mountain. Under us the huddle of tents beside the lake loses size. Down the valley the first small trees shade green.

J.L.'s eyes are wide and she's laughing out loud. Thompson is busy pointing out landmarks to her. And all of a sudden I realize that she doesn't like cooking or washing dishes so much. She didn't come up here for that. She's so excited I figure I'll give her a thrill. When we rise to top the ridge I shove the nose up. The helicopter loses air speed, moves more and more slowly. Just beyond the crest I cut over and let the throttle speed take us in a wild plunge almost to the floor of the valley below. She gasps but she loves it. She's not afraid at all.

Farther up the next valley we find a bare spot to drop Thompson and Mackenzie. They get out and crouch, holding their hats and their packs down against the wind from the blades. "Come and sit up here," I holler back at J.L. In a moment she's buckled into the seat beside me and we've lifted off again.

"Can you do that again?" she shouts.

I motion for her to put on the headphones, so we can talk.

"What?" I grin. I know what she means.

"Climb up and then drop down like that."

"Oh that. Hang on."

I take her into a real hammerhead stall. The kind that usually scares the hell out of anyone who hasn't flown in a chopper before. You climb steady until you start to lose air-

94

speed, until you're almost stalled, then you swing the nose around and power dive. I've had guys who were so scared their knees buckled when they got out of the chopper. Not her. She hangs on but she loves it, she's laughing like crazy all the way down. I feel a little ashamed that I didn't offer her a ride before. All those trips during the day when I could have taken her along. Especially since she loves it so much.

I do a few tricks on the way home. Nothing dangerous. She gets used to it fast, knows when I'm going to swing over and dive. "Had enough?" I finally ask.

She laughs. "It's great, but I suppose I should get to my dishes."

I turn the machine back toward camp, cruise down the valley to cross the mountain. Then, far below us on the gray-ish tundra, I see a huge brown spot that seems to be moving. And sure enough, it's running, lumbering along. I point it out to J.L. "Look, a bear."

I take the machine down, fly a little closer to the ground. And then I see. It's a grizzly, a huge goddamn mother grizzly, and running behind her are two cubs, doing their best to keep up, but losing ground all the way. She's too fast. That huge, unwieldy body is moving with more grace and speed than a horse can run.

When we're almost above her she puts on her brakes and stops. Slowly she raises herself on her hind legs and stands there, immense, reaching for the helicopter as if she will pull us out of the sky with her raking claws. The two cubs are still running to catch up, small cinnamon bundles trundling across the moss.

Beside me, J.L. strains forward.

"We've disturbed her valley," I shout.

"God," she breathes. "That's her. She's incredible."

I turn the machine and fly away. No use making her mad. "Yup, you wouldn't want to meet up with her in a dark alley."

"Where will she go?"

"Into the next valley."

"But we're in the next valley!"

"I expect she knows that. With two cubs she won't plan to visit people."

"Imagine," says J.L. "Imagine her being like that. Imagine!"

"Yeah, it sure helps in a fight."

She grins at me then, as if she hasn't been listening for a moment and missed a joke.

Back in camp she says, "Thank you. I really liked that."

"Any day the chopper isn't full."

"Thank you," she says again and smiles at me like a little girl before she jumps out and runs for the Jutland.

The way the two of them like flying, her and Thompson ought to get together.

Jerome

The little bitch gets her own way about everything. She's got Cap hauling her water and burning her garbage, she's got Ivan giving her rides in the helicopter. Thompson's even washing her dishes when he's supposed to be working on the maps. Everybody's doing her work for her and what the hell does she do all day? Women. They're nothing but trouble. No matter how you treat them, they always want more. You've got to let them know who's boss right from the start. That's Mackenzie's problem. He doesn't say a word to her about anything.

And her cooking. I can never tell what the hell I'm eating. Practically need a road map to get through it. She puts garlic in everything, even my piss smells like garlic. She does bake half-decent bread but if that's all she can do, I say she's not worth it.

And she doesn't try to get to know the crew. Hardly talks to them, goes to her tent the minute she finishes her work at night. Sometimes she'll have a drink, but she never has more than one. Thinks she's just too damn good. Well, one of these days one of those guys is going to get mad and give it to her. And I won't be the one responsible, I won't have anything to do with it. It won't be that she doesn't deserve it either.

Stupid bitch. Sometimes I catch her looking at me with a smirk on her face and I'd like to wipe that expression off her mug once and for all. Wait until Mackenzie goes out. Then we'll see who's boss.

And him, he's sure got a bee in his bonnet. He's killing himself, combing these claims like he expects to find gold or something. Isn't satisfied with the radiometric survey, he's got to get a sample from every boulder and ship it off to be assayed. The only way you find anything is with a scint or a spectrometer. He just figures he's going to make me look bad, dumping fifty pounds of rocks out of his pack every night. Oh, I know he's good, he works hard. But finding Meteor Ridge improved his position a lot. The best geologists aren't always the ones that find a mine. It's luck mostly. He doesn't deserve his reputation, he's no better than the rest of us.

Mackenzie

Radiometric survey:

1. Scintillometer grid — measure total radioactive counts.

2. Spectrometer survey — measure uranium counts.

3. Electromagnetic survey — run perpendicular to strike check for conductors.

Uranium potential?

Thompson

I can't understand what she does out there. We're working away on the scintillometer grid and I see her orange rain-suit moving up the cirque. She walks along light and easy, and when she gets to the point where the mountain starts to slope upward more steeply she stops, gets down on her knees and starts digging in the ground. After a moment she gets up and walks a few paces, then kneels again. Interesting. What is she doing out there, digging around? Maybe she's bushed already.

I'm the one who should be bushed. This grid is so boring. Put the scint next to the ground and take a reading, walk to the next station. Walk, walk and walk some more, rain or shine. I want to get out on reconnaissance. Smash some boulders. If only I could get a small beep out of this scint. Another fifty meters and no goods.

Milton

Every day dirt bagging like mad. Dig a hole six inches down and fill a soil sample bag. Walk fifty meters and do it again. Every hole has a number, you write the number on the bag and pack them all up and send them off on the airplane. What can they tell from dirt? Thompson says it's geochemical analysis, but it's only dirt. Grainy and dry, not like the topsoil at home, the way it smells cool and dark when you turn it up behind the discer. And at prayer meeting the men have black moons under their nails and the women's faces are scrubbed wind red under their dark kerchiefs, and even the church smells like earth.

Every day that girl. She should be called Fern or Amanda but instead she has a name like a man, J.L. She doesn't drop her eyes when you stare at her, just stares right back.

At night after supper I run, I have to run to keep things straight, I race over the uneven ground until I am run out of myself and I can breathe steady and even again. If it's not that girl I can't stop staring at, then it's them drinking liquor while they draw on the maps. I hear their voices low and muffled inside the lighted square that is the tent. Their rumble reminds me of men eating after a day working together, someone's crop maybe, and the women serving pork chops and apple sauce and pudding from the kitchen where they chatter high and soft, and the girls blushing when they come to stack the plates.

They prayed I would not come here. They told me there would be men drinking and bad language and evil thoughts. I was ready. But they said there were no girls up here. You don't kiss a girl until after you're married.

Hearne

I've only managed to get a few photographs of her. A couple the day she learned to shoot the rifle, but they're of her back, she looks just like one of the men. And another, when I came into the cooktent one day and caught her as she raised her head from the batter she was stirring with the wooden spoon.

In the picture her face is unsurprised but guarded. She's arrested there, head raised as if listening. And her eyes, gray-green malachite, pierce unwavering. Under the slanted brim of her hat they penetrate the very picture itself. When I got it back that picture jolted me, the unearthly knowledge in her eyes. I tried to give it to her, but she would barely glance at it.

"Keep it as a souvenir of Fort Chaos," she said. "You'll never get a cook as good as me again."

"Brag, brag, brag," said Cap derisively. "Cooking isn't everything."

And I put the picture away. I don't like to look at it, but she won't pose, won't stand still for the camera. It might be the only one I ever get of her.

Hudson

Between the religious kid and Jerome I'm ready to blow my bloody head off. At night I drop onto my cot like a stone and I don't even dream, I sleep solid until she starts banging that damn gas tank at six-thirty. You couldn't sleep through the din if you tried.

It's the mountains. Sure, the helicopter drops you off in the morning, but you've got to walk until he picks you up again. And me, I'm walking behind Jerome, he carves out these big bloody samples and makes me carry them. The more Mackenzie brings back, the more Jerome figures he should bring back. Except that Mackenzie carries his own rocks. He's a good chap, but I wish he'd see that Jerome is slowly killing me, and I don't dare say anything or he'll make it that much worse.

Besides, the geology here is unreal, so complex it's almost impossible to figure out. The age references do nothing but confuse me. These rocks have mineral compositions that I've never seen in England. And Jerome won't explain, he just tells me to use my head.

I've never felt so far from the world. It's damn primitive, that's what it is. I thought the cook would help, be a softening influence, but she's as savage as they are. She'll laugh and talk but carefully, like she has her guard up all the time. Not much comfort. And she can't brew a decent cup of tea, just makes that foul black coffee, so bitter it makes you retch.

The mountains. They'd never believe it back home. They're so rugged a man could never get anywhere alone, he'd die before he had a chance. No civilization, nothing. Even the airmail letters from home are crumpled and torn by the time they get out here; sometimes I can hardly read them. Probably nobody in Mayo can read. I'm sure they've never heard of Cambridge.

Roy

The tension is plain as can be. They like her plenty but they keep their distance. It's gingerly respect. And I can understand it. When I motor up to shore and see her standing there with that hat tipped over her eyes, I'm not so sure either. An innocent face can hide a mean streak.

I just hand over the groceries and the mail. Sometimes I stay for coffee, but it's more to be polite than because it's comfortable. I can see those guys aren't suffering, they're not losing any weight. But not one of them's got through to her yet, I can see that too. And it's not for lack of trying. Cap looks at her like she's a melting ice-cream cone. She ignores him.

I have to chuckle. Last time I came they had some wild story about a grizzly bear. That prick Jerome is walking around waving a handgun and bragging about what he'll do if he runs into the bear. Talk about obnoxious. And it's easy enough to notice that he has a real hate-on for the cook. Hope I don't get called to fly out any casualties. She better be able to take care of herself.

Mackenzie looks tired and distracted. Poor fellow's been at this game so long you'd think he would give himself a break, but he's driving himself harder than ever. He must have the patience of a saint, running this camp. The crew gets worse every week. By the end of the summer you can commit them all.

J.L.

I should have seen it coming. But I thought that if I ignored him, if I pretended not to notice, he would leave it alone. Stupid of me, after all these years I should be prepared. But I wasn't. Cold rain for three days straight, the tent dripping, the men dripping. Breakfast, dishes, baking, dishes, supper, dishes. Mackenzie absentminded, Jerome sniping at me, Franklin either asking me to read his poetry or describing the color of my aura, Hearne with that pesky camera, Milton staring at me all the time. About the only normal one is Thompson. So when Cap comes in and makes his announcement like he's being funny, I'm hardly in a mood to be funny back.

"I'm horny."

"So?" I say, rinsing cutlery.

"You're responsible," he says with a silly grin on his face. Cap reminds me of nothing so much as a comic-strip character, complete with freckles and a cowlick.

"If you weren't here, I wouldn't be," he says.

Just like a man, blame a woman for everything, even his hormones. I want to tell him that masturbation is a nice solution, but instead I shake my head and scrape at another plate. "Cap, you're a nice boy, but I'm not interested." Hell, that was no good, I want to be firm and direct and instead I sound condescending, superior.

And it makes him mad, I can tell by the way his tone changes to threat.

"J.L.!"

But between the dishes and the rain and the never-ending scrutiny, I'm losing patience. "Cap, if you're goddamn horny, go find yourself a grizzly bear."

That does it. He stands there and curses me up and down, calls me a cocktease and a bitch, a useless cunt, on and on and on until I feel like I will scream, even though I'm pretending to ignore him, studiously drying dishes in an effort to block him out.

When he finally gives up and stomps out, I start to shake. I put the towel and the plate I'm drying down, I edge myself onto a chair and lay my head on my arms and cry, let myself cry for the first time since I came.

I want to go home. I want to get out of this plagued camp, I want to go home to Deborah and the men I can predict. I'm tired of being weighed and watched and judged and found wanting every minute of the day. I thought I could be alone here. Instead, I find I'm less alone than I've ever been. Here I'm everyone's property, I belong to every one of these men.

Cap

There's something the matter with her. I've tried, I don't know what I'm doing wrong, but she's not interested. She just looks at me like I'm a post or something. I haul water for her and I burn her garbage and she doesn't say a thing, acts like she'd rather do it herself. On nice afternoons she takes off and heads up the valley, and when I ask her where she's going, she just shrugs.

Damn. I tell myself to forget it, she doesn't like men, probably a lesbian or something. But when I walk into the cooktent and she's bent over, pulling apple pies out of the oven, and she straightens up and shoves that hat back on her head and grins at me, I get warm all over again. I can't figure out why. She's flat as a board, a nice bum but no boobs at all, and she has those high cheekbones and a wide mouth, you can't even say she's sexy, let alone pretty. She sure can't afford to be choosy.

Me, I'm not so bad. I'm short but I'm good looking, not one of these lumberjack types. And hell, I don't walk in here at six o'clock sweating like a pig, socks so rank from those damn boots they're almost ready to rot off. I'm the most likely guy in this camp. Ivan's around in the day, but shit, he's in love with his helicopter. I told myself to wait and see, she's got to get lonesome sooner or later, but we've been out here three weeks now and she doesn't even flicker.

So I decide to ask her. No harm in that. I walk into the cooktent after everybody's left one day and I stand there, waiting for her to say something. She ignores me, she's washing dishes with a furious intensity, slopping them around in the soapy water and then throwing them into the rinse water pail with a splash.

"J.L.?"

She doesn't stop. "What?"

"I'm horny."

"So?"

"You're responsible."

But all she says is, "Cap, if you're so horny, go find yourself a grizzly bear."

And she won't talk to me after that, ignores me even when I tell her she's not fair, she's a cockteaser. Stands there and dries dishes with a look on her face like she's a million miles away.

I swear at her and leave, no use even talking to the little bitch. I might as well stand in the rain and help Ivan fiddle around with his helicopter.

But if he hadn't seen it too, I wouldn't have believed my eyes.

We're working away, talking, when something makes us both turn around at the same time and look down toward the Jutland. There's a faint haze of rain and for a moment I'm sure I am dreaming, I have to blink to focus on what I see. And then I cannot move, I am absolutely pillared in place.

J.L. stands beside the cooktent, perfectly relaxed and easy, and facing her, twenty feet away and reared up on her hind legs, is a huge goddamn grizzly bear. J.L.'s face is tilted up and the she-bear's face is tilted down and they're looking at each other like they've met before. And then J.L. sweeps off her hat and bows at the same instant that the bear seems to shrug, and drops to her feet. For a moment more they stand there as if in conversation, then they both turn. J.L. goes back into the cooktent and the bear lumbers away down the valley. From behind the corner of the tent two little cubs scurry to follow her. She ignores us completely.

When she's far away I turn slowly, dare to look at Ivan. His face must be as white as mine. "Did you see that?" I whisper.

"Jesus, yes."

"What the hell. . . "

108

He puts a hand on the helicopter to steady himself. "She's a witch," he says hoarsely.

Together we walk over to the cooktent. When we lift the flap and enter, she's peeling apples and whistling under her breath. We stand there and look at her.

Finally Ivan says slowly, "Was that a grizzly bear?"

She flicks a piece of peel from the paring knife into her mouth and smiles. "Yes. And by the way, Cap, she said to tell you she was available if you thought you were up to it."

Ivan looks from her to me and back again. She keeps peeling apples and I can only stand and stare at her.

"Are you all right?" he says finally.

"I'm fine," she says. "Why?"

He shakes his head.

She laughs, grins at both of us and says, "You want some coffee? It's on the stove."

Hard to believe. Impossible to believe.

Ivan

What did the she-bear tell you, J.L.? What did she come all the way over the mountain to whisper in your ear?

J.L.

I knew her. She came to me in the she-bear. She came to me and she reared herself up big and beautiful and wild and strong and she said, "Wait. Don't let them drive you away."

I clench my fists. "I'm tired, I'm so tired."

"Just stay," she says.

"But one wants to murder me and one wants to fuck me and one wants to take pictures of me, and what are the others going to want? I thought it would be different out here."

"You thought you'd leave all that behind? There isn't a place in the world without it. You can try to escape, but it's better to face it head on."

"I'm ready to give up, lay them all one after the other, let them do what they like with me."

"That won't help."

"Who cares? What am I, some kind of sacrifice?"

"We all are," she says. "We all are already."

And then she's gone, with the two squealing cubs tumbling behind her. Leaving with me her smell, her invocation, the power of her long, curved claws.

The first time I saw her she was singing. She had on an orange shirt, I remember that flagrant color. She held a tribal drum between her knees and she was singing with only her fingers on the drum to accompany her. It was very strange and very beautiful. I was there with a man, of course, some man who'd made a mess in my kitchen that morning. I forgot him. I was arrested, hooked by her. And I don't remember her being beautiful that first time, I only remember the exquisite timbre of her voice. That voice could make shape of chaos, give tongue to every inarticulated secret and intuition. I loved her. At that moment I wanted to abandon men forever.

Of course I didn't. One doesn't easily give up a centuries-old habit. And she wouldn't let me. She had men herself, needed them as I did. Except that for her it was so much more difficult, so much more complicated. They paraded her first for her beauty and then for her voice, they worshiped her, proposed to her, presented her. And ignored her. I saw it instantly, the circle of admirers with eyes fixed on her face, men with no ears. I had to push my way through them to get to her, elbow my way between the tweed jackets and monogrammed shirts. She still held the drum, as if it would protect her.

When I was finally standing in front of her, I was tongue-tied. She looked up at me and did not smile and it was then I saw the loveliness of her face.

"Thank you," I said. It was all I could manage.

She gave no more sign than a quick tightening of her lips, as if even that were dangerous, before the men closed in again.

I thought that was all, that I'd seen her and then lost her. But she looked for me, she hunted until she finally found me in a grubby university cafeteria. I didn't recognize the person who sat down across from me.

"Hey, remember me?"

I shake my head.

"Come on." She opens her mouth and sings, just a line, a bar, just enough to remind me.

"Oh!"

"I've been hunting all over the place for you. I knew you had to be at this university, but you do stay well hidden."

I shrug. "I'm not crazy about this place."

She reaches out a hand and touches my arm. "I wanted to say thank you for coming up the other night. It's never happened before. Women don't like my songs."

"You scare them."

She sighs. "I don't mean to. I'm only trying to sing what I feel."

"That's a sin. You're supposed to sing our tradition and history and structure. The cerebral."

"But singing *is* visceral."

"It used to be."

"To me it still is," she says fiercely. "Sorrow or celebration, that's where it all came from."

"Haven't they tried to turn you into an opera singer?"

"Oh, I've already proven I could do that. They're quite fascinated by my rebellion. Except that they all want to claim me."

I laugh. "I noticed."

And so I played cynic to her songstress. I went to all her concerts with whatever man I had at the moment and watched the other men cluster around her. It became one of our habits to meet afterward and discuss them, those men. If they only knew how viciously we satirized them, they would have buttoned their pretty black jackets with dismay.

We became friends, we shored up our injuries, we celebrated our winnings together. And what a friend. The kind who gives spice and laughter to everything around her. Beautiful but never vain, the only thing she takes obstinate pride in is her voice, her deep valley of a voice. While her music gets stranger and she begins to lose even that captive coterie, my life grows more remote, secluded, and I want only to get away from the telephone, the bed, the growing chain of men who rattle and clink behind me.

"Why so many?" she asks me one day.

I look at her sharply. She's never said anything to me until now. "I'm looking for a good one."

"Oh J.L., J.L. Just save yourself."

"How many have you tried?"

"Three," she says steadily.

I laugh harshly. "A twenty-five-year-old woman who's only made love to three men?"

She nods miserably. "I can't bring myself to do it if I don't care about them."

"If you care, they'll destroy you."

She says nothing, only sits with lowered head.

But I go on, realizing myself what follows. "And if you don't care, you'll destroy yourself."

She looks up at me with her eyes full of tears and then we are holding each other tightly, breathing together, her hard curves pressed against my bones.

Old she-bear. Tell me what to do.

Jerome

This camp gets worse all the time. Now everybody's telling bear stories. According to Ivan and Cap, the cook practically kissed a grizzly sow. I don't believe it, they say that bear was only twenty feet away from her, but they've got to be crazy. There's no fucking way you could meet a grizzly with two cubs and not be mauled to death. It was probably miles away and turned around when it smelled the camp. Bears aren't interested in messing with humans. And if the old sow is, we'll see how she feels about my Magnum. I hope I run into her out on the slopes, I'll finish her off quick.

J.L. just says yes, she saw a bear, and Ivan and Cap sit there with their eyes bugged out. They must have been into the booze. Or else they were smoking dope. I'm sure Cap has got some hidden away that he brings out when Mackenzie's not around. We've got to make a rule in this camp that everybody stays sober. It's going too far. At night all they do is sit around and drink, play cards, and the next day they're useless. If they're this bushed now, what are they going to be like in two months? And Mackenzie doesn't say a word to them.

As for him, he refuses to believe that this uranium deposit is any good. He's wasting half our budget assaying for other minerals. And he won't listen, hardly asks my advice at all. Instead of concentrating on an EM survey, he's already planning further exploration. I think we should stick to the property. At least we've got something to work with. Maybe I can persuade him to let me handle the property while he takes care of reconnaissance. Brilliant — I could save the program!

Thompson

She's kneading bread on the flour-sprinkled oilcloth, her arms pumping steady and even, the dough moving like it's alive under her hands. I dump my pack outside the tent and slump down in one of the chairs.

"You're back early," she says.

"Didn't wait for the chopper. I walked."

"Long way."

"It's downhill. The only bad part is contouring across that talus slope."

She has molded the bread into neat loaf shapes and is putting the pans on top of the stove to rise. The tent is filled with the rich, yeasty smell.

She rinses her hands in the dishpan and says over her shoulder, "You want a beer?"

"Sure."

"I'll go get it."

I sit there and soak up the smell in the tent, the warmth that she's made here, and I know I'll never be able to eat payella or curry or chili or smell bread baking without thinking of her.

When she comes back with the two bottles, wet from the lake, she grins and gestures at the beer still sitting on the crossbar of the tent. "You know how often I swear at that bottle?"

"Quite a lot, I'll bet."

"It was a good idea. The other day I was almost ready to take the first plane out."

"Cap finally made his move."

"How did you know?"

"I could see it coming. Funny, it's usually the helicopter pilot who's trying to get it on with women. They're the ones who have this romantic aura surrounding them. That fancy machine and they're always a little cleaner, not quite as sweaty as the rest of us."

"Ivan doesn't bother me."

"No, he's sensible. He likes to fly."

"Isn't it something? Riding over the mountaintops like that. I wish I could fly one of those things."

"He's let me try but it's a lot harder than flying an airplane, really difficult to maneuver."

"I love it," she says wistfully. "Swinging over the valleys. Almost as if you're in a cradle that some enormous hand is carrying through the sky."

"Why don't you take flying lessons?"

"Huh! Where would I get the money?"

"You'll have all the money you earn this summer."

"That's supposed to send me back to school."

I look at her. "I didn't get the idea that you were going back."

She shrugs. "I don't know yet. What alternatives are there?"

"Become a helicopter pilot. You'd probably have to carry your nets in the machine to stabilize your weight, but there's no reason why you couldn't do it."

She laughs then. "You are crazy, Thompson. I had enough trouble getting a job as a goddamn cook!"

"You did it."

She looks at me and I swear her face softens. For the first time since I met her, she's dropped that damn porcupine shield.

"Well." She takes a swig from the bottle. "Nice idea, anyway."

I've been waiting for a moment like this, hoping that maybe she could try to get through to him, break that black preoccupation of Mackenzie's. "Hey, J.L.?"

"What?"

I hesitate. "Do you think you could try and talk to Mackenzie sometime?"

Her face hardens and I sense her drawing away. "I talk to him all the time."

"I don't mean, 'Do you want some coffee? Do you want ham sandwiches? Do you want gravy on your potatoes?' I mean, talk to him about himself."

"What for?"

"J.L., I've never seen him like this. There's something wrong. He's not happy, not the way he used to be."

"It's none of my business."

"I know, but maybe he'd talk to you."

"I'm not here to play counsellor. I'm here to cook."

"I know, but Christ, J.L., he won't tell me anything. I've tried."

She shrugs. "He seems okay to me."

"He's not. And it's more than just the fact that this stupid property is a bust. It has something to do with him."

She shakes her head. "I'm sorry, Thompson, I'm not going to meddle. What do you think I should do? Walk up to him and say, 'Hey, Mackenzie, I hear you have a problem. Want to talk to me about it?' No way. I mind my own business."

I sigh, finish the bottle in my hand. I can't say anything else. Maybe she'll think about it some more. "J.L.?"

"What?" she says, and I can tell she's mad at me.

I stand up and give her a quick kiss on the cheek, so quick she doesn't have time to protest. "You're a good cook."

"Beat it," she says. "If you can't stand the heat, get out of the kitchen."

Ivan

I'm no heavy sleeper but I didn't hear a thing. Slept better that night than I've slept since I got out here. Terrifying, when you don't even feel disaster, death flashing past. But nobody woke up, we all slept straight through. It frightens me that not one of us sensed something.

I was flying the chopper. Rotoring over an endless range of mountains until I came upon a deep, rainbowed waterfall. I took the helicopter down and hovered there, just above the foaming water, held it so that the spray stippled the bubble, held my machine in the middle of what became a perfect color-refracting prism. Until the prism splintered and we crashed, the chopper twisting to metal sculpture around me. I've always dreamed that I'll be killed flying.

J.L.

I felt the mountain rumble, I felt it stir and I was instantly awake, listening with every bone arched. Silence, perfect silence, taciturn and patient. I raise myself on an elbow, turn my head to catch the resonance of the camp. They are all lost in that deep labyrinth of sleep, dreaming. I button my shirt, slide into my jeans and take my hat outside into a wide night with a blazing moon. Under my bare soles the moss is warm, elastic. I move through the huddle of tents leaving no footsteps, no stirring. To my left there's a long deep snort of breath and I smile, knowing that the sound is not Mackenzie but Jerome. He would snore.

To my right is the Jutland, my kitchen, resting in anticipation of tomorrow's pancakes, of tomorrow's soup and salad and fried chicken. I run a hand along the canvas wall as I pass. In the firepit a few embers still redden the black, but they're silent, unhissing. The fire has become a ritual, these men worshiping Phoedima's god and never knowing it. And now I'm clear of the camp, moving up the valley. The cirque rests at the neck of the mountain, it creeps upward, lifts itself to a ridge and then ascends the crest. That mountain hovers, holding itself against the moment of upthrust time that left it there to wait. We haven't given it a name, but from the camp we look up to it, always we lift our eyes to its peak.

And I put back my head and look up to that jagged stone crown waiting all these thousands of years. I move to balance myself so that my feet are planted firmly, take a deep breath. Silently I call, the invocation blossoming from my skin, my sorrow, the very spaces in my bones.

Behind me the camp wears a veil of silent mist, separate. Then through the soles of my feet I feel again that spasm, the earth gathering herself. It shudders deeply once, and far, far above me I hear the splash of a pebble bouncing from a cliff.

The sound seems to fade but then it's joined by the smaller chinks and spatters of stones, a trickle that gradually cascades to a small stream gathering earth and shale and rocks, begins to sing, to surge, to roar, and finally to rumble, to thunder immense and savage, tearing pieces of the mountain's granite with it, boulders tumbling over themselves in heavy consternation, the whole side of the mountain caught in a torrent of itself, sliding in heavy loss down its own flank.

I stand there, rooted to the sound of the cataract, hear it growing huge and loud until I can see that gray wall of stone rushing down to fling itself against the gentle curve of the cirque. But it doesn't stop, it carries itself down the cirque toward me, its thunder crashing in my ears, so close I cry out in terror, hold my palms against it roaring over me, my body ground by rocks. It rumbles itself still then, the slow echo of an enormous letting go. I hear a stone roll not ten feet away, and in the after-silence I finally dare to open my eyes. My feet are still planted steady in the moss, and the moon is still brilliant and unclouded. But the mountain. The east side has let go and slid down into our valley. Where once was an even slope rises a raw gap.

I kneel then, press myself down and whisper, rock myself and whisper softly until the earth and I grow still, calm ourselves.

And they didn't hear it. When I finally slip back to my tent, they're still dreaming. Men with no ears, men with no connection to the earth.

Mackenzie

Slide: the descent of a mass of earth or rock down a hill or mountainside. I remember the definition so well, but I've never had one practically rush over me.

On my way to the cooktent one morning I stop dead. The whole side of the mountain has slid down into our valley. We were a hundred yards from being hammered to death by boulders. One by one the men come up and stand beside me, stare wordlessly at the tons of rock and debris. Ivan walks over to his helicopter, gleaming yellow paint in the sun. Even Jerome is silent, white.

Finally J.L. appears in the door of the cooktent. "Hey," she yells, "aren't you guys going to eat?"

We turn and file into the tent, into the smell of buckwheat pancakes and warm honey.

"Didn't anybody hear it?" I say finally.

They all shake their heads, dumb.

"I did," says J.L.

"You did?"

"Yes. I saw it."

"And you didn't wake us up!"

"There was hardly time to move camp," she says dryly, flipping another pancake.

"What time was it?"

"About two-thirty, three."

"What were you doing outside?" asks Jerome belligerently.

She looks at him. "I was relieving myself."

"Well, what happened?" says Cap.

She shrugs. "I heard a rumble and then the whole damn mountain came tumbling down."

"You saw it all?" says Thompson, incredulous.

She nods briefly.

He whistles. "Boy, I'd rather sleep through it than see it coming for me."

"It wasn't coming for *me*," she says. "More pancakes, anyone?"

I can't believe it. In all the years I've been up north, I've never had such a strange thing happen. To sleep through tons of rocks crashing not a hundred yards away! And J.L. Either she's lying or she's got piano wire nerves. It's strange. Why did she hear it when we didn't?

"When are we moving?" says Jerome.

"Why should we move?" I ask. I have to stay calm.

"I don't exactly want to get crushed in my sleep."

"Well, it's slid now. It can't slide any further. No point in moving."

He glares at me, superstitious and afraid.

"Look," I say. "We were lucky. We're not going to move, we'll go on with the work as planned."

Half an hour later I'm almost ready to climb into the screaming helicopter when I stop dead. "I forgot something," I holler and run back to the cooktent. J.L. is wiping down the table.

"Hey," I say, "did you really see it?"

She nods, then bites her lip and turns away.

"Why didn't *we* hear it?"

"I don't know."

I stand there, angry.

"You think I wasn't afraid?" she says.

Of course. Of course. A small girl with nine men sleeping behind her watching half a mountain crash down at her feet. And I grab her then, grab her by the arms and shake her a little. "I'm sorry. I'm stupid. You were right, if you'd woken us up everyone would have been running around having fits. You were right. I'm sorry."

And she's crying, she's standing there with her fists clenched at her sides, crying. So what can I do? I wipe her face with my sleeve and raise her chin. "I'm sorry."

She wobbles a smile then, so I shove her hat down over her eyes and run for the waiting helicopter.

Mackenzie, you've got to find a mine, or this camp is going to blow sky-high.

Cap

The summer gets stranger and stranger. First she hits right in the middle of that target, even though she's never shot a gun before. And if I hadn't seen her talking to that bear with my own eyes, I wouldn't have believed it. But I did, and so did Ivan. I wasn't imagining it. Then she sees a rockslide that stops just short of camp. Even worse, the rest of us don't hear a thing, just sleep right through tons of falling rock that practically roll right over us. Unbelievable.

Yet when I'm on the radio to Mayo this seems like any other summer, any other camp I've been in. It's her that makes the difference, it's her. I never would have believed it.

She's a witch, I swear. I should leave her well enough alone, if I'm not careful she'll hex me. Even so, I would like to get her clothes off. I'd like to see what she can do underneath that cool skin. That she's so strange makes her even more interesting. I wonder what she'd be like kneeling above me, working over me with that bony little body of hers.

How does it feel to screw a witch?

Thompson

The men are spooked, uneasy, they look over their shoulders without warning. The rockslide frightened them, sleeping through it absolutely oblivious to the mountain roaring down on us. I can't understand why we didn't hear it. I can't explain why J.L. did. But I know one thing. This is the Yukon.

The Yukon is a magic place. I know it, Mackenzie knows it. It's a place where reality is inverted, where you have to take strangeness for granted. There's nothing usual or ordinary about this camp. Nine men and a girl living in tents, a thundering machine that drops us off on a mountain slope every morning to scout boulders for something valuable, uranium, silver, gold. So how can we expect the ordinary?

And maybe she is magic, maybe she did invoke that mountain down on us. Then again, maybe she stopped it, maybe she stood in its tracks so it couldn't reach us. It's possible. It's there in the solitary way she goes about her work, unblinking, her quick twists of humor, her face reflected by the patterns of the fire. She centers this whole summer for us.

And she cooks. Every night we have something more unusual. I'm sure we haven't eaten the same thing twice. Even if it's steak or chicken, it's done a different way every time.

One day I come in and she's standing there, hands on her hips, swearing at the beer bottle over the door.

"Damn you," she says. "Damn you anyway."

"Hey, what's this foul language?" I say as I step inside.

She grins. "Coming from the cleanest mouth in camp."

"What's the matter?"

"Oh," she shrugs. "Everybody treats me like a jinx, as if I'm responsible for that rockslide. I can't help it if you guys sleep like treetrunks."

I laugh. "You're providing the most interesting summer we've ever had."

She doesn't deny responsibility. "I just cook."

"Hey," I say, "things will settle down again. Pretty soon everybody will be bragging about it."

And it's true. The only thing to do is keep going, keep walking up and down the slopes, keep hammering, keep packing rock samples. The uranium property doesn't look so good, we need to find something more. Jerome insists the assays will be high, but Hearne says the results of the radio-metric survey are poor, low-level uranium, small patches of high intensity, but not enough to warrant excitement.

We need to find something else.

Roy

When I fly in with the supplies that Wednesday, I hardly recognize the place. It's as if someone bombed the side of the mountain. I wonder if they're still alive, but when I edge in to the shore, they're waiting as usual.

"Oh yeah," says Cap casually, reaching for the mail bag. "It was pretty spectacular."

"A little hair-raising, wouldn't you say?"

He shrugs and grins. "We need some excitement now and then."

They must be really bushed. And no wonder, most crews get out a couple of times during the summer, but these guys don't seem to be going anywhere. Three months in the Yukon mountains would drive a saint mad.

And it is Fort Chaos. Every week the camp seems less stable. I can't describe it, it's more a feeling I have, but it's getting so I'm glad to get out of there, glad when my floats lift off the lake and I'm buzzing back to Mayo.

That cook just doesn't change. She's as cool, as secretive as ever. I think she's got the whole camp by the balls.

Hudson

This place is damned, doomed, at night I can't breathe for those mountains out there. Jerome pushes more and more, he'll hardly take ten minutes to stop and eat lunch, he's always charging ahead of me. There were lots of chaps like that at public school, always have to prove they're better than you. Snivelling scuts. Never thought I'd end up running behind one.

Bloody hell, but this country is barren. I hardly dare to think of the way England will be green now, the way the country lies soft and lush under the summer rain.

And Milton, every night he prays harder. I'm not sure who'll crack up first, him or me. I don't even mind the kid anymore. He listens to my woes about Jerome and sympathizes. And as long as I don't bother him about religion he lets me alone. It's better than bunking with Jerome, he'd probably tell me whether I should sleep on my back or on my side. Bastard.

Mackenzie

Did she think she didn't matter?

Some things don't hit a person until it's too late, until long after you should have thought of them. All these years I spent just thinking dully that she left and never trying to think why. Or how hard it must have been. She would have been frightened, terribly afraid, I knew her enough to know that. She could grit her teeth and carry something off, but she'd worry, she'd edge and fret around it first. Until I'd get impatient and tell her to do it, stop dithering and just do it.

And it must have been like a rockslide to her, the suddenness, the enormity of it. One small trickle of pebbles taking half a lifetime with it. I'll bet she was surprised at herself, making a move like that, stepping over a cliff.

I'm not proud of myself. I did all the wrong things. Hired a private detective, hunted everywhere myself, acted like she was a runaway teenager. And staying in that house, pretending to be faithful, pretending to be noble by being there just in case she came back. Was outraged when she wouldn't take money. I hounded her, she probably had to move a hundred times because of me. Still, she won. I've never yet managed to find her.

The only good thing is that I never accused her of leaving me for another man. At least I gave her that much pride. If I'd used that as an excuse, I couldn't look myself in the face now. I still don't understand exactly why she left, but I can finally see it as something that she did, a decision that she made, an act she carried out. That is the hardest thing to face, the rockslide of her intention.

At least this summer has taught me something. When I get home I'm going to sell that house.

Ivan

After the slide, everything goes downhill. It's been raining for a week. Cold rain that chills you right through. Puts everybody in a foul temper. When I fly the men out, the helicopter is full of curses and the smell of steamy rain suits. And the mist. It obscures the mountains so that I'm flying on a wing and a prayer.

At night everyone's wet and muddy and snarling. They drink more. In the morning they're late getting up. J.L. keeps an impassive face but she's wary, watchful. She knows she's liable to get it first.

Mackenzie won't quit. Hands out orders every morning like he's blind. And Jerome tries so hard to be tough. He won't say anything. Only Thompson looks worried. The men don't dare to complain around Mackenzie, but Thompson hears everything.

The seventh morning is the worst. When I come in for breakfast, Hearne is jabbing his fork at Franklin. "You were talking in your sleep again, you scum. If your meditation relaxes you so much, why do you yell in your sleep? Every night you wake me up."

Franklin takes a slurp of coffee and says to Mackenzie, "Why does Cap have the radio in his tent? He's supposed to do the sched in here. He's just too damn lazy to get out of bed."

The kid Milton has his head down and is shoveling eggs in so fast he's going to choke. Hudson is holding his head, as if he has a hangover.

When Jerome comes in, he says to J.L., "I want bacon."

"There isn't any," she says. "It's sausages today."

"I hate sausages. I want bacon."

"Well, you're not getting it," she snaps.

131

"You little bitch, you're supposed to cook what you're told."

She ignores him and stabs a sausage with her fork.

Jerome starts to move toward her but suddenly Mackenzie stands up and says quietly, "Everybody shut up."

He stands there, looking around at the crew until they are all quiet. "Looks like we're getting a little bushed," he says finally. "We'll have a camp day today. After breakfast you can either soak your head or go back to bed. Just make sure you're in a better mood tomorrow."

And sure enough, that night we're in better spirits than we've been for two weeks. Everybody cleans up and supper is like a party. Afterward we sit around the table drinking and laughing and telling jokes. Even when she's finished the dishes and made the lunches, J.L. doesn't go off to bed. For once she stays, lays out a game of solitaire.

Jerome is telling stories about all the assistants he's had. I wouldn't work with that bastard for anything. Knowing that you'll become one of his jokes. Poor Hudson. Only Mackenzie doesn't seem to be listening. He's working on the big map.

"You know," says Jerome, "my best assistant was the one who created the biggest problem."

Hearne pours himself another shot of rye. "What was that?"

"Well," says Jerome, "it's a long story." He leans back in his chair and smirks at us. "He was a good kid, he'd do almost anything. If you told him to climb a vertical cliff, he'd climb it. If you told him to cross a roaring stream, he'd wade right in. Never complained, never asked any questions, just did what he was told."

"He was crazy," says Thompson.

"No," says Jerome, "he knew his place."

"So what was wrong with him?" asks Cap.

"Well," says Jerome solemnly, "he had a problem."

"What?" Cap is getting impatient. "Hey, Franklin, pass the bottle down here."

132

"He fantasized," says Jerome, looking at each of us in turn. "He fantasized."

"So?" says Cap. "We all fantasize."

"Well, he got a little carried away."

J.L. raises her head. She is slowly turning a beer bottle between her hands.

"Everybody that comes out here gets carried away," I say.

"No, he was different. He was a good assistant, he adjusted well to living in a camp with a bunch of guys, he got along with everybody."

"Sounds like a bloody saint," mumbles Hudson.

Jerome ignores him. "But he fantasized." He takes a swallow of beer, the beer that Thompson brought. "There were about six of us sleeping in one tent. It was crowded, but we didn't mind, we were used to roughing it. About ten we'd all hit the sack, we were getting up at five, so we'd be pretty tired. The first night I was almost asleep and I heard this funny noise, like one of the guys was having a nightmare or something. Well, after some thrashing and heavy breathing, he stopped and I went to sleep, didn't think anything of it. But the next night it happened again, and the night after that. Except it was getting worse, louder and longer and he was moaning and carrying on like crazy. I didn't really want to say anything, so I tried to ignore it, but it sure kept me awake."

"Sounds like you, Franklin," says Hearne.

"I don't have nightmares."

"But you shout in your sleep."

"Well," Jerome continues, "this went on for a week or so and finally the crew started to complain about it. They said it was my assistant making all the noise. So that night, right on schedule, sure enough he starts snuffing and moaning. I have to do something, so I holler, 'Jim, wake up!' The noise stops for a moment. 'I'm awake,' he says, and after about thirty seconds he starts again. I sit up. 'Jim!' Well, he just sort of groans and goes right on thrashing around on his cot.

And suddenly I realize that the guy is masturbating, he's having himself one whale of a jack-off. Well, that embarrasses the hell out of me, so I shut up and lie back, but of course I can't get to sleep until he's finished."

J.L. is watching Jerome like he's some kind of snake, but the rest of the crew is snickering and making comments. Milton looks like he's ready to bolt. Only Mackenzie pretends he's not listening.

"This goes on every night until finally the crew starts getting pissed off. They yell at him to shut up, they throw their boots at him, but he just keeps right on. Seems like he carries on for two hours before he finally falls asleep. And then, of all things, he starts waking up at two or three in the morning and doing it again. That was the last straw. It's one thing to have a guy beating himself when you're trying to get to sleep, but it's quite another to be woken out of a sound sleep by a guy moaning and groaning."

"What did you do?" asks Cap interestedly. Milton is sitting there red as a beet.

"We had to banish him," says Jerome. "Nobody was getting any sleep at all, so we threw him out. He had to sleep outside."

"I don't believe a word of it," says Thompson.

Jerome shrugs. "Believe it or not. We called him the mad masturbator. Too bad. He was a good assistant."

J.L. stands up and bangs the kettle on the stove. "Poor kid," she says.

Jerome swings around and glares at her. "Listen, that's why you can't have women in camp. Can you imagine what he would have been like if there'd been a girl around?"

"Oh come on," says Thompson. "Don't be stupid. Maybe he wouldn't have done it if there'd been a girl around."

"Maybe he would've been worse," says Jerome.

"Maybe he couldn't sleep," says J.L.

Jerome shrugs. "Too bad," he says with a smirk. "A guy's got to learn to control himself. Well," he stands up, stretches, "I'm for bed. You guys put that bottle away and hit the sack. You've had your day off, you better be ready to roll tomorrow morning." He goes out and walks away, whistling.

Hudson thumbs his back as he leaves. "No wonder the poor chap masturbated," he says glumly.

Mackenzie suddenly swings around from where he is working at the drafting board. "Is he giving you a bad time?" It's the first time he's paid attention to anything but work for so long we're all startled.

Hudson lowers his head, shrugs. "No, not really. He complains at me a lot."

Mackenzie studies him. "Well, as long as it's just talk. If he starts pushing you around, let me know."

Hudson is embarrassed. "Aw, he's okay. I'm just not used to working in the mountains."

"Hmmm," Mackenzie says. He starts rolling up the map, looks at the crew like he hasn't met them before. He moves his gaze all around the table until he gets to J.L., standing by the stove. He looks at her for a minute, then he sighs and says, "Anybody got any scotch? I'm dry as a bone."

J.L.

Men are like children. I remember Deborah telling me that, but I never realized it before, not like I know it now. Looking around the table, I think how unripe they are, how they cover everything with a layer of bad jokes, laughter.

Except Mackenzie. Thompson is right, he's upset about something. Every once in a while he presses his fingers to his eyes as if it's not maps he's seeing. But what can I do, the longest conversation I ever had with him was in the hotel room after I told him I was a girl. All I can do is stew and simmer and stir and serve and wash dishes.

If he would only laugh. I haven't seen him laugh once, not in the whole month we've been here. That jolts me. Maybe I could make him laugh, make him think of something else besides that dogged idea that has its teeth sunk in his heels. I'd like that, I'd like to see his face open, I'd like to see him lose that preoccupied expression, I'd like to see him raise his head from those everlasting maps. He's been fair, he's given me a chance.

And I'm fine. This summer isn't what I expected, but I'll survive. That's what we are, after all, we women. Survivors. Thank God for the she-bear and Deborah, or I would be back home right now and Jerome would be strutting around saying, "I told you so!"

They're finally coming clear to me. At first they were just a mass, a clot of men, all of them watching me, pulling at me, indistinguishable. But now they're separating into themselves, distinct male people.

Mackenzie most persistently. He was the clearest to me from the start. Maybe because of me seeing his cock like that, or him mistaking me for a boy. I feel like I know him better than the others, almost as if there's a secret between us. He's so quiet here, but so very much in control, directing the work, running things smoothly, yet he pushes himself harder than anyone. Tall, stooped, brown hair almost ready to turn gray. His clothes don't quite fit him, he must buy them himself. And that odd vulnerability that shows through his careful alignment with his work. He loves his work, he loves rocks and maps and the way the earth has given birth to herself. He's an explorer, a discoverer of abundance, and a man who knows enough to be awed when he finds it. The rest of them swagger, pretend, carry the subconscious belief that six inches of ludicrous, dangling flesh gives them strength, power.

Like Jerome. If he can't shoot it or fuck it, he's not interested. That's all you can say about him.

And even Thompson, likable as he is, has that sheen, that patina of presumption, unquestioned right. Maybe he'll lose it yet. He's still deciding, still on the edge. Small and compact, he's full of mischief and laughter. There's a sensuality to his movements, to his mouth; I sometimes think that if I touched him I could feel the current that runs under his skin. He's the only one of them that seems sexual to me, the only one I can imagine responding to.

Poor Cap. Always thought of himself as a lady's man. He can't understand what he's doing wrong. Restless, he's always looking for the next smart move to make. You can't turn your back on a man like that, he's quick as a rat, not so harmful but still, a rat. I imagine him with a ferret face, pointed teeth. If you cornered him, he would bite.

Not like Ivan, slow and stolid and gentle, who looks at people from under his duck-billed hat and is bewildered by them. He likes the intricate fittings of machines, the way metal parts slot into each other, the steady, even roar of a motor. His one ability is flying helicopters; apart from that, he's totally ordinary, he does not analyze.

While Franklin analyzes everything, over and over again. He takes equipment apart just to see how it works and then cannot put it back together. Last week he almost terminated

Cap's radio. He's growing a scraggly beard, he writes bad poetry, he meditates, his life is a long course in self-improvement. Conversion too. He's convinced that he has answers, that by going into a corner every two hours and sitting cross-legged with his eyes closed and his fists clenched, he's going to alter the course of reality. I can't think what kind of a geologist he is, he does his work but he seems to have no connection to the rocks at all, not like Mackenzie and Thompson do.

Hearne is better, but still, he can see things only if he fixes them forever in a photograph. He likes colors, textures. I've seen him touching the most ordinary things as if discovering their surface. Dreamy and absentminded, dark eyes hidden behind heavy glasses, swarthy and enclosed and secretive.

Not like Hudson, living on the edge of hysteria. The poor guy is so nervous he can hardly hold a cup, he fidgets and fusses and irritates. Typical long nose, long face, long teeth. Upper-class British prep school, impeccable accent and manners, but he's going mad here, he's afraid these mountains are going to get him. And if the mountains don't, Jerome will.

But if Hudson is homesick, that kid Milton is having culture shock. Every time one of the men says "fuck" he turns scarlet, every time they bring out the cards and the bottles, he leaves. And if I burn my finger and say "hell" he looks at me like I'm the whore of Babylon. Tall, gangly, awkward, doesn't have any control of his limbs, I can't let him near my kitchen corner or he's sure to knock something over. I feel sorry for him, he seems to have led such a cloistered life until now that I wonder how he'll deal with this rupture in his world. The ambiguity of religion: giving you something to believe in but making you use that belief to contend with the world. He hasn't had much to do with women. He stares at me all the time, his eyes follow me everywhere.

All of them sitting in a circle around this table, listening to Jerome. Snickering like small boys. Except for me, it would be a men's poker night. Only Mackenzie doesn't listen. Mackenzie doesn't laugh. His back is turned, he has his map spread on the drafting board and is drawing intricate contours, formations.

That beastly Jerome. Complains about everyone drinking, but sits here drinking the beer that Thompson bought. Telling some crude exaggerated story about a kid masturbating when he knows damn well that every man in this camp does it. And he enjoys himself. The sadistic bastard loves to embarrass Milton, he loves dominating Hudson, he knows he can get away with it.

I would like to take him down a peg, he gets cruder and cockier and more miserable every day. The men don't like him either, they distrust him, ignore him or edge around him.

And suddenly I almost chuckle out loud. I've got an idea.

Thompson

Ivan and me are sitting on the edge of our cots, having one last cigarette and talking about flying when there's a footstep outside the tent and J.L.'s voice says softly, "Knock, knock?"

I'm in my shorts so I jump into my sleeping bag and Ivan says, "Come in."

She rasps the zipper open and ducks inside, acts like she always does this. "Hey, are you guys in bed? Listen, I've got a great trick to play on Jerome!"

Ivan laughs and I sit up.

"Wait a minute," I say. "I know we'd all like to see the bastard hanged, but there's no point antagonizing him."

"He has to be able to take a joke. It's just funny, it's not mean." And she lays it all out for us. Before she's even finished, I catch myself grinning. It's a great trick but it will make him hopping mad.

J.L. looks at me for approval. "Okay?"

"What the hell. It's harmless enough," I say.

She beams. "Okay, I'll call you in the morning. Remember, keep it quiet."

And I hear her in the darkness going from tent to tent, hear snorts of laughter and then the low rumble of voices, she is setting up everyone in the camp. She visits every tent except Mackenzie and Jerome's. I'm not worried about Mackenzie, he'll know right away it's a joke, but Jerome will probably kill us.

As she slips back past our tent, she sticks in her head and hisses into the darkness, "All set. Hudson wasn't too keen, but I talked him into it. Even Milton said he'd be there." She chuckles once and is gone. I hear the zipper on her tent and then silence.

"Thompson?" says Ivan.

"What?"

"J.L."

"What?" I know he is trying to say something personal.

"She — " He hesitates and I wait.

"I like her," he blurts finally. "She's weird, but I like her."

I raise myself up on one elbow. "Ivan, listen. She wants to learn to fly."

"What?"

"She wants to learn to fly but she's scared, she thinks she can't do it."

"Helicopters?"

"Of course. Airplanes are baby stuff after you've been in a chopper."

"I don't know," he says doubtfully.

"Come on, Ivan. Why not?"

"She's pretty light. I don't know."

"At least she could try to find out about it. If you told her it wasn't so hard, if you talked to her. . . "

"Yeah," he says slowly, thoughtful.

I lie back then, stare up into the shallow darkness of the tent. Around me the camp whispers, the wind lifts a tarp and flaps it once, then there is quiet. She wants to fly, I can feel how much she wants to. And I see an image of her in the helicopter, face shaded through the glass, holding that stick. And we're flying, flying over mountains bleak and gray and suddenly the flying turns into Katie dancing, her body caught in mid-air, in a double turn, suspended — flying.

Jerome

She hammers that goddamn tank so hard it almost lifts me straight out of bed, she takes a bitchy delight in it, I know. Goddamn cooks, always feel superior because they get up before you do. Well, I never lie in bed and wait until the last minute, I'm always one of the first ones in for breakfast. Yesterday she refused to cook me bacon, but we'll see about that this morning. It's time somebody started nailing her down. She gets away with murder.

Mackenzie's up already, stepping into his pants. What a grouchy bastard he is, doesn't say a word in the mornings. I get dressed quick and head on down to the cooktent, but even before I get there I can smell the bacon frying. All the more reason to give her hell, yesterday she said there was none. I push through the tent flap and then stop dead in my tracks.

J.L. is cooking breakfast all right, but the whole goddamn crew is still exactly where they were last night, half lying, half sitting, dead drunk and pissed to the eyeballs, so loaded they don't even stop grinning when they see me. Those assholes have been on an all-night bender. All the bottles are empty, Hudson's asleep on the table, there's cards spread all over. Jesus!

Thompson is the first to see me. He hiccups, covers his mouth. "Mornin', guvner."

"What the hell is going on here?"

Hearne winces. "For Chrissake, don't shout."

"What?" I roar. "You guys are all fired! What the flying fuck do you think this is, staying up all night drinking and playing cards?"

Cap yawns. "Is it morning?"

"You're damn right it's morning, and you're going to get your ass out on that mountain if I have to kick it up there!"

"Not me," says Ivan. "I feel sick."

"Jesus H. Christ, I have never seen such a useless crew. You guys couldn't find a playboy bunny if she was hidden under your bed."

"Where?" says Cap and looks under the table.

Just then Mackenzie steps into the tent. He looks around at the men, then at me. "Who's getting fired?" he asks quietly.

"Every last one of these motherfuckers. They can't pull this kind of bullshit!"

For a moment he looks gravely at the crew, then his mouth twitches. "All right, guys, that'll do," he says.

I can't believe it. He isn't going to do a thing, he's going to let them get away with it!

"Goddamn it to hell, Mackenzie — "

And suddenly the whole crew sits up and starts laughing, even Mackenzie, laughing and laughing, and I swing around ready to punch the first one, and Mackenzie grabs my arm. "Hey, Jerome, calm down, it's a joke."

"Joke!"

"They set us up," he says, grinning.

Those bastards, those goddamn two-bit bastards. I'll bet she put them up to it.

Mackenzie

You should have seen his face. When he finally caught on I thought he would swallow his tongue. I couldn't help laughing, it was so perfectly clear that they'd carefully arranged themselves to look as drunk and sleepy as possible. They didn't tell me they were going to do it, but I knew the minute I walked into the tent that it was a set-up. Serves him right, maybe now he won't ride them about drinking. Although I know he has a dangerous temper, he'll try to get back at them somehow.

And of course he blames J.L., says she put them up to it. There she was, frying bacon like crazy and trying not to crack a smile. Serves Jerome a plateful of it as sweet as you please and he can't say a word, he asked for it yesterday.

He rants and raves for a while all right, calls everybody's parentage into question, until Thompson says coolly, "Hey, what's the matter, Jerome, you can't take a joke? Mackenzie laughed."

"It's not funny," he barks, but he shuts up, he can't argue with that logic.

And the whole crew is pleased as can be with themselves. They put away the empty bottles and eat a huge breakfast. The rain has stopped, it looks like a good day, sunshine and a breeze. Every one of them feels good, you can tell by the way they stomp around and make fun of each other. And Cap, cocky little bugger, says slyly to Jerome as he's leaving the cooktent, "Hey, Jerome, want a quick snort to start the day?" Jerome glares at him and follows. Outside I hear him haranguing Ivan about getting dropped off first.

I unroll my map on the drafting board and have a look at what I want to cover today. So far, even with the rain, we've done well. And I have to admit, Jerome's idea that he take care of the property work while I do reconnaissance is a good one. Keeps us both happy.

J.L. is whistling and clearing the table, putting the plates in the dishpan. She works inside this space as if she belongs here, as if it's part of her. I turn and watch her for a few moments and I have to smile. It's inconceivable to me that I could have mistaken her for a boy, she is every inch of her female, marvelously light and easy and quick, carrying the mystery that is only there in women. Because women are so mysterious, so blind and inward and silent, so tuned to vibrations that we have never been able to hear. They turn in faultless circles, they move like vases forming, always changing but always perfect. And even J.L., slight and angular as she is, has the fluidity, the deep swirling motion of water.

Now she's up to her elbows in dish suds, only stopping once to shove her hat back on her head. She doesn't notice me, she's wrapped in her own world far beyond me. And suddenly it occurs to me that she could tell me, she could explain what Janice wanted. I stare at her then, feel that cold emptiness of not knowing, of loss. But how can I ask her, how could I ever explain the situation to her. Impossible.

She senses me watching because she turns, smiles over her shoulder. "If you're looking for your lunch, Mackenzie," she says gently, "it's on the shelf. I put in an extra apple."

That's when I realize that she knows more than I imagined, she carries inside her a knowledge that is endless, frightening, some way of catalyzing sorrow to joy. Her face before me blurs, for a moment I think she must be transforming herself in front of my eyes, but then she's only J.L. in her cotton shirt and blue jeans and running shoes, scrubbing at melmac plates with a sponge.

"J.L."

She turns and looks at me again, her wet hands falling to her sides. Her eyes are starred, wide periwinkles of that indefinable green that can change so easily to blue or gray.

Caught then, I feel that if she could only look into my eyes long enough, I would be transformed, transfixed by her sphere of knowledge. But I cannot bear it, I stumble, fall away from the radius of her gaze. I have to turn.

"You're doing a good job," I say brusquely, rolling up my map with hands that almost tremble. "You're the best cook I've ever had, just like you promised."

She laughs then, soft and happy, comes to stand beside me. When I turn she is so close. And she doesn't hesitate, puts her arms around my waist and hugs me, hugs the whole length of that bony little frame against me, with so much love and gentleness that I can hardly see to stumble through the door.

Hearne

You should have seen his face. I only wish I had taken pictures, it would make a hilarious photo-essay. And the way he carried on! It was too funny, we'll have something to laugh about for days. And J.L. acting like she was totally innocent, when she was the one who thought it up.

Sure picks up the old spirits. And today is the first clear day for two weeks. Far in the distance you can see snow on the mountain peaks. Maybe if I get high enough today, I can get a few photographs, there aren't many days up here when you can see for miles. The last pictures I took were of the rockslide, and I'm sure they'll turn out flat and gray, no way to see the awesome texture of the rocks that have choked up the valley.

If I could only talk J.L. into letting me take a few shots of her. I'd like to do a series called "bush cook." The contrast with all the men would work so well. She hates having her picture taken, she's stubborn. Just the other day she swore at me for hanging around her with my camera.

"Go and take pictures of the scenery," she said, "not me. I'm here to cook, not pose for you."

But if I could only have a chance to take a few of her, I know I would find the perfect picture, the one I've been trying to get for years.

Milton

Every night now we have a fire, we gather sticks and burn them together with the garbage. It's eerie, the sparks against the solid darkness. The mountains lie uneasy after the slide, they're not peaceful and far like the prairie is. I miss the prairie, the unrolling land.

When I get back home, I'll stay, I'll wander no more. There's nothing for a man up here. Everyone sits around the fire, but it gives me a lonesome feeling, I miss church, young people's meeting on Wednesday, choir practice on Friday, seeing everyone the same.

I'm here now more than a month. They're careless, they aren't Christian, but they're good, some of them. Mackenzie and Thompson mostly. The rest of them are talk, they puff themselves. Hudson is afraid, I want to tell him about Christ, but he's afraid and doesn't want to hear.

And that girl, that cook. She looks at me, she dares me. I never seen a girl's eyes like hers, just asking you to say something to her. She makes me feel scratchy and bad, like I've done a sin just looking at her. Girls, all the time girls. It's them that makes you do dumb show-off things, it's them looking at you makes you itch. And their faces so quick, one moment quiet and the next pursed and silly. I'll marry Hanna Friesen. It will be a few years yet, but she's slim and swaying under her dress, she doesn't look back at me but she knows. And then when you're married you can. That is why you wait. Stand up in church and say yes, or you're doing a sin.

I have not kissed a girl. You cannot kiss a girl until after you are married.

J.L.

And now their shadowed faces ring the fire in a perfect circle. They are all of them becoming lucid to me, crystallizing into themselves and yet they are all men, all and every man I've known, I've stroked, I've taken. Not one took me, and there have been enough who tried.

I know, I admit, I confess, I have been loved only too well, and I have felt little guilt for my own lack of desire, my passive body acquiescing to touch but moving only for myself, not another. Oh I have loved in return, but never quite to the furthest reaches of possibility. There is always a remnant of desire left. Although it should not be a competition, I compare. Their movements, their hands, their nerve, their own reactions outside mine.

I have sometimes thought that I should make a list of all the men who have made love to me, who have labored over me in some predestined effort to arouse beyond all others. Although I could make a list of details, I could never range their faces side by side. There is no clear face, only shapes of faces that transform themselves to shadows when I peer more closely.

I do remember certain parts. No, not their cocks, although I have stared at enough in an effort to understand the male scepter. It is their feet that never fail to amaze me, their feet that I remember. Hardly an object of erotic interest and yet as much a signature of the man as his name. If I feel a spark of tenderness for a man, it will be because of his feet. The variety is endless; narrow fragile feet, splayed and crooked feet, broad competent feet, quick intelligent feet, neat meticulous feet, kicking furious feet, mathematical thoughtful feet, smooth feet and feet with toes that carry tufts of hair, bogey-man feet, careless laughing feet, graph and slide-rule feet, Bible-thumping feet, paper and pencil feet, suffering victim feet, logic philosophy feet, telephone directory feet, executive washroom feet, achieving immigrant feet, proud assuming feet, feet that wear brogues and sandals and ski boots and oxfords and tennis shoes and grips and hiking boots.

Some of them even tried to make love to me without taking off their socks. Who was it, that famous Indian described as having small neat feet. Oh yes, Almighty Voice. Perhaps that is why he's known as such a fine lover. I can tell how the cocks will perform by the feet. A man who will not let you touch his feet is afraid of women.

Thompson

It was her idea to have a fire at night. We pile up the day's garbage and as much scrub wood as we can find and let it burn. It's different from sitting inside the cooktent, we're a circle against the darkness, against the wolves that pad softly beyond the outer rim. There are timber wolves in the valley further down, in the trees. I saw them one day on traverse, four of them that followed and watched me with a dispassionate curiosity. They are muscled, huge, I can see how when they yawn one jaw touches heaven and the other touches earth. The wildlife this year has been oddly shy, uninterested in the camp. Aside from J.L.'s conversation with the grizzly, we've been left alone, no bears digging in the garbage, no mice, even the ground squirrels are quick to disappear. It's as if they see us and veer away, as if they have been warned. Perhaps they are wary because of the slide, sense its danger.

The summer is half over, we're a crew now, we know each others' habits and ideas, one body. The work is going well. Mackenzie and I are doing reconnaissance work further out. Soon Jerome will finish that electromagnetic survey; the whole grid has been sampled.

Sitting on the spongy moss with the fire wavering across my face, I feel again that quiet, time held and stopped right here. On the other side of the flames, J.L.'s hat shapes itself, for a moment her face flares white and then falls into shadow again. After the slide she has somehow become our center, we all orbit her. There's the work, but that's simply what we do. We look to her for focus. And she stands quietly within our circle, unafraid to bend us backward upon ourselves.

We look to her as if she has the power to transform. Something makes you want to tell her everything, spill yourself for her. She never seems to listen, but she hears, she absorbs us through her skin, through the tips of her fingers. And all she does is cook, mix and simmer and bake.

Now, around the fire, we are one voice rising and falling, a group of men in unison with the bony shadow of a woman weaving a spell. I still miss Katie but she has become less shaped, more an image that I see caught in the figures of her dance. I open the letters she sends and I read the round, childish handwriting, and even while I feel an ache for her, I find her distant, remote. It happens every summer. When I get home and find her flesh again, I am always surprised at her solid density. I want to tell J.L. about her, want to see if giving words to her will maybe make her seem more real. But I'm afraid; it seems presumptuous of me.

Mackenzie

"Sex," says Cap one night. Just like him to bring that up.

"Sex what?" asks Hearne.

"It's missing. We've got everything else. A roaring fire, mountains, the moon, the wilderness. It reeks of romance, except no sex."

"That's not exactly what a person comes up here for," says Thompson quietly.

"Well," Franklin shifts back on an elbow, "when the bears start to look good — "

"Ground squirrels would be easier to catch."

"Reminds me of the one about the Australian sheep farmer," says Cap. "He finally got so lonely he started in on a sheep and all his friends stood around laughing because he picked the ugly one."

Everyone snickers, but J.L. coughs and says softly, "It's been done."

Instantly we are silent, we strain to hear her.

"That's an old story," she says. "You're not being original at all."

For a long moment we wait, held in a hiatus that hesitates outside the fire's circle. And then her low, storytelling voice.

"Zeus once fell in love with a very beautiful girl, whose name was Io. Now, Zeus' wife, Hera, was jealous of his many affairs and watched him closely. One day, when he was flirting with Io, his wife came looking for him. In order to feign innocence, Zeus changed Io into a heifer. But Hera knew that Zeus couldn't possibly be interested in a mere heifer and demanded the creature as a gift. What could Zeus do? If he refused, she would know that the heifer meant something to him, and so he was forced to give his beloved mistress to his jealous wife.

"Hera set Argus, with his one hundred eyes, to watch over Io until Hermes (sent by Zeus) lulled Argus to sleep and killed him. Then Hera sent a fly to torment Io. She knew this was no ordinary heifer that her husband found so fascinating.

"Poor Io. Imagine being turned from a beautiful young woman into a cow, feeling yourself a haired and hoofed and horned beast simply because of the intemperate lust of a god. Inside her beast's form she must have mourned, she must have lowed and kicked in resentment. And it was only when Hera extracted a promise from Zeus that he would leave Io alone that she could be returned to her human form. When she was, Zeus had to keep his promise. Ironic, that he was only allowed to love her while she was a heifer.

"And once," J.L. goes on, "there was a writer who wrote a very strange and awkward story about a man who loved a cow."

Jerome's snort is cut off as if someone has dug an elbow into his ribs.

"He loved that cow to distraction, he watched for her, he followed her, and finally, because it wasn't his cow, he stole her. People thought this man was an idiot, but although he couldn't speak very well, he loved immensely. He loved that cow. And when he finally found a barn for her, he made love to her. What else could he do? How else could he show her? She let him.

"The problem came with other people. They were outraged, they laughed at him, they watched him, they sold tickets. And in the end, to save themselves and their meager reputation, they killed the cow and fed him a piece of her meat, thinking that would cure him of his irrational and fatal attraction. Of course, some of them made a tidy profit in the process."

Around the fire there is absolute quiet, the men lean slightly forward, pulled into a motionless circle they have never imagined. J.L. talks as if they're not present, as if she is only telling herself a well-known story.

"And once there was a writer who wrote a very strange and beautiful story about a woman who loved a bear. The bear was a tame bear, but he was a bear, a big furry beast. He made love to the woman, he licked her in such marvelous and intricate ways that she was satisfied as she had never been satisfied by a man. But of course he was a beast and when she forgot that, he reminded her. Strangely enough, her love for him made her clean and good. And that love was neither frustrated nor killed, but allowed to stand in its own time and place when both the bear and the woman went on with their lives."

The men seem hypnotized, frozen against the light that licks from the flames. There is a long piercing silence.

"And that's better than your story about the farmer," she says.

"Whew," says Thompson finally. "How did we get onto this?"

"Sex," says Cap. He hasn't heard a word.

Thompson

Afterward they're quiet, she has silenced them completely. The fire hisses and sings, begins to sink to embers. One by one they slip away, they yawn elaborately and stretch and say, "Well, I guess I'm off to bed." Until it's only me and her sitting there, not close, a hummock of moss between us, but together. Usually she's the first to go to her tent, but tonight she gazes abstractedly into the flames as if still lost in her own story.

Finally she sighs and says, "I guess I overdid it. Shouldn't try to reform people."

"No," I say. "It was a marvelous story. But you've got to realize they're a little afraid, you see through them so easily."

"Afraid?" she says.

"Sure. Women are these hidden, inexplicable people. Here you are cooking unimaginable things, handling everything so calmly, keeping so cool. And then you tell a story like that!"

"Thompson, are you afraid of me?"

I laugh. "Only sometimes. Hey, one last drink?"

"Sure. Might as well."

I move closer to her, pass the rye bottle. She tips it up, takes a swallow, passes it back to me.

"You know," I say, "you've been good for us. I was in a camp with a woman before, but she was a geologist and she was so bound and determined to prove that she could work as hard as a man that she overdid it."

J.L. groans. "We get it coming and going."

"Oh I know, I know it couldn't have been easy for her. But she was so rigid, just wouldn't relax. So determined to show us her competence that she was no person at all."

"And my competence?"

"Have you had any complaints about your cooking?"

"Only Jerome."

"He doesn't count. If the men don't complain, they're happy. You could probably get a job cooking again next summer."

"Do you think Mackenzie will keep on doing this?" she asks.

"Coming out in the field? Of course. It's his life." I stare at her. "Why?"

"I don't know. A feeling."

"He seems to be more positive. He was unhappy at the beginning of the summer, but I don't think he'll abandon geology."

"What makes you guys do it?"

I take my time answering. "The barrens. Going to places where nobody's been. The possibility of finding a mine." I gesture at the fire. "This."

"Is it enough?"

I draw back, she has hit something I've always skirted, rocks and the mountains and Katie and my life somehow all tangled up together, and then abruptly I'm leaning toward her, spilling everything, Katie dancing, Katie needing me, Katie, Katie, Katie, me wanting the mountains and the rocks but afraid that I'll lose her, I'll have to trade her for my work, should I marry her, should I try to take her with me, should I expect to lose her? Somewhere in my blurting she has put an arm around my shoulders, she is holding me, listening quietly, immobile face reflecting the last sputter of the fire.

When I stop I feel I've let something loose, all the hopelessly knotted snarls and tangles of the things I want.

"How long have you been together?" J.L.'s voice is beside my ear.

"I met her seven years ago. We've lived together on and off for five."

She nods. "When you go home in the fall, do you try to take the bush with you?"

"What do you mean?"

"Do you try to cram the mountain in your duffel bag?"

I laugh. "Literally? Of course not. I take enough samples, but I can hardly take the whole mountain."

"Because you can't, right? Well, you can't take her up here with you either."

"But if I could only be sure of her. I've asked her and asked her and she won't get married."

"Would that make you feel better?"

"Yes, it would. At least I would know she belonged to me."

She says nothing for a long, long moment. Behind her I can see the jagged and tumbled shapes of the rocks from the slide. Finally she sighs. "Thompson, I know you won't believe me, but you could marry her a hundred times and she would never belong to you."

"But if I only knew she. . . "

"Why do you have to know? Did you know there was going to be a rockslide? Did you get killed?"

I'm puzzled. "No."

"Knowing won't make any difference at all, because you can only know something the first second you realize you know it, and after that the knowing is only a memory of knowing. Things change. Be happy with her when you have her, be happy with the mountains when you're here."

There is something hammering inside my skull as if she has struck at the one answer I never wanted. "But how can I live like that, never knowing from one day to the next whether she'll be there when I come back?"

"Ask Mackenzie," she says.

"What?"

"His wife left him. He has all the earmarks of a man who always believed his wife would be there when he came back. One day she wasn't."

"How do you know?"

She shrugs. "He's learned the hard way. If you don't expect to keep Katie, you'll always be happy if she stays."

I sit up and stare at her then. "Just go on the way we have?"

She looks flat into my eyes, the outline of her face pale. "Why not?"

"Do you love anyone?" I finally ask her.

She laughs and stands up, flexes her knees from sitting in one place for so long. "I love a beautiful singer," she says, screwing the cap on the rye bottle, then handing it to me. "Here. It's time for bed."

J.L.

And after they leave I run myself a tub full of water as hot as I can stand and lie there as long as possible sloughing them off, dissolving the sweat, the spit they've chafed into my skin. It's their smell that lingers. Although I soap and soak I can sometimes smell them three days later, abandoned with me the thick and clotted scent of their whispered intercourse.

They practice that so well, lying on top and pouring lies into my ear as a cover for the stroke stroke stroke of their cocks. And if once I rouse myself to stare up into a face, actually look at them, I am only horrified, repulsed by the blankness, the distance evident there. They are not feeling me, thinking of me, working over me. It is any or every woman that they hold in their arms, their expression as withdrawn and distant and inner-directed as if I was not even present. It's then I want to shock them out of their complacence, erase their blindness and assumption, hammer them into the ground.

And in the end, exceptions prove the rule. There have been one or two who saw me, J.L., person inside my body; it's them I try to remember, the ones that held me between the light and the shadow, suspended me in that terrific hiatus between one movement and the next. For them I could come and come. Those men roused me by acknowledgment, their lack of fear. But even they were fleeting, quick to disappear. Nameless now, in the myriad of others.

Milton

I said I would not kiss a girl unless. I said I would not. Girls all the time laughing and walking with skirts flattened against them in the wind. And talking, their voices moving up and down, now whisper disappeared, now shrill. Their skin if you could touch it is like touching grass, it slips away between your fingers.

Playing hide and seek between the granaries in the wheat chaff, dark rustles and running footsteps.

"Ten, nine, eight. . . Ready or not, I'm coming."

If you look up to the lip of the sky the dark is thinner. Crouching to see if they are under the hay wagon, I catch a glimmer in the corner of my right eye and instantly I'm running after her, flying braids and skirts and elbows and scraped knees. For one second I feel the sprigged material of her dress on my fingertips and then she's hammering the granary door with her fist. "Home free!" And turns panting to face me, her lips slightly drawn over white glistening teeth. I want to strike her, girls aren't supposed to run, that's why they have skirts. She cheats, bunches them up around her waist, if I told her mother she would get the switch. But I don't know how to talk about skirts.

All of a sudden I want to kiss her, I want to press my sweaty face against her, I want to feel those teeth under my lips. I stare at them, wet, parted, her tongue between them until she laughs and gives one last thump to the granary door with her palm, sidles away. "Home free."

That was when I knew I had done a sin, wanting to. And so on Sunday when we knelt on the floor, elbows on the pews, I prayed to be saved from badness and I swore, I made a vow that I would not kiss a girl, I would never kiss a girl unless I really meant it.

Ivan

She flies with me a lot now. Almost every day. If I have room in the helicopter I tell her. She'd never ask. But all I have to say is, "Want to come along?" and her face lights up, she drops what she's doing and she's ready right there. Riding along, she'll ask me questions about the machine. Questions about how a helicopter flies. What it can do. She starts to learn the instrument panel and pretty soon she knows what everything is for. But when I ask her if she wants to try the stick, she shakes her head. "No."

Sometimes she says nothing, just sits beside me while we dip and swing over the mountains. She puts a tape on and we'll both have the music thundering and crashing in our ears above the lower vibration of the machine. She loves that. She'll close her eyes and just listen and fly.

The crew like it when she's with me. She always has her pockets full of something. Apples, mountain gorp, nuts. Or a joke. I think she makes them up, those stories. But the guys love it. One day she told some crazy backward variation on the princess and the pea that had Thompson and Mackenzie killing themselves in the back. Jerome just sat there looking sour.

They're working further out now. There's only about six weeks left and I guess they haven't found much yet. Mackenzie says the uranium property is marginal and that he can easily find something better. Jerome says the property has potential and that Mackenzie will never find anything better.

I like to have her along. It makes me feel safer. She's got luck. When she's with me in the machine, I never get that panicked feeling that suddenly everything will explode on me. It's the one thing they don't teach you in flying school. How to stop being afraid of the fatal mistake you're certain to make one day.

Mackenzie

One day we find something. Thompson and I both start to notice small blebs of arsenopyrite in quartz veins. We don't say anything, but we hammer every boulder apart, carry enough samples so that we can't possibly be mistaken. The rocks have a grayish metallic luster and under a coating of my spit they glint back the sun.

We spend a long and careful day, angling across the side of the mountain. Neither of us says much. Best not to say anything until you're absolutely sure. You can only send the samples in for assay, bag them and label them and wait for the results. I used to get impatient waiting, knowing I had found something good. Now I figure it isn't going to run away.

Thompson is excited though. "What do you think?" he says when we're waiting for the helicopter to pick us up.

I shrug. "Can't tell with these fine-grained rocks."

"It looks good," he says tentatively.

"Seen lots of things that looked good and didn't turn out so good. Like the uranium property we're sitting on. Sure, there's uranium there. But it's not enough and it's not high grade enough."

"But, Mackenzie, what if. . . "

"Hold on, hold on. Don't get ahead of yourself."

He stares down the valley, eyes narrowed against the sun. I can almost see the visions in his head.

"Hey, do we have some good sharp axes? Start some of the crew cutting posts." And that's the only satisfaction I'll give him, although it's enough to make him beam. Nothing beats a staking rush for excitement.

Even me, I still get that prickle in my blood when I think of staking what I know is a good property, hammering it into two post markings so that you know it's yours, you've got it.

A small showing wouldn't be a bad thing at all.

Jerome will be furious. He insisted on staying with the property work; he's still convinced that uranium is the best prospect. And he could be right. There's something there. He's working at it hard enough.

Waiting here, leaned up against a boulder to rest that heavy pack of rocks, I feel something rush away from me, a weight, a seal on my days broken. I can be happy. Sky, rocks, the mountains, maybe even a mine. Janice is gone. It still matters to me why she left, but the going itself is finally over.

Then the helicopter nears, a soft thudding in the distance that grows louder as it clears the ridge behind us and hovers down to settle on an even patch of ground. Thompson and I grab our hats, duck, run for the machine. J.L. is in the front seat beside Ivan.

"Hey," she says over the headphones when we've lifted into the air again, "did you guys find a goldmine or something?"

We look at each other quizzically.

"Why?" says Thompson.

"You're both beaming."

"Oh you, you're imagining it." And he knocks her hat over her eyes.

Thompson

Strange how after I told her everything about Katie and me I feel relieved, emptied out. She treats me just like before, doesn't mention it again. I like her better every day. She's the kind of person that you want to stay watching, moving like a silver fish between us, all we men trailing in her wake.

Everyone feels cheerful except Jerome. He's more doggedly determined than ever, for what, I don't know. The man baffles me. He seems to want to do everything against everybody else, in opposition to. Maybe it's the property, but he is black-humored as a snake. I'm waiting for him to do something drastic, to fly into a rage any day now. Poor Hudson. I hope he doesn't get it in the neck.

Soon the big chiefs will be coming through on their annual tour. I hope Jerome doesn't pull anything then. Although I suppose Mackenzie can handle it, he's been with the company so long he isn't afraid of the bigwigs. I hope we have something good for them — if only the assays on the showing are high. Gold. I hardly dare to breathe the word.

Funny that J.L. guessed like that. Every night now on my way to bed I stop by her tent and talk to her for a few minutes, sit on her cot and have a drink of rye with her to top off the day. I didn't notice at first, but she has moss drying all over the floor of her tent.

"I guess you're no rolling stone," I say.

"Why?"

I gesture.

"Oh," she laughs. "I like the smell of it. Peppery and sweet. Like nothing else I've ever smelled. This summer would be worth it just for the tundra moss."

"Not the men?" I joke.

"Oh, some of them. I liked the rockslide. And the bear.

I like flying over the mountains in the Jet Ranger." She stands up and hands back my bottle. "Go to bed, Thompson. I've got to hit the boards at six to make French toast."

Cap

She's impossible to figure out. She's as friendly to me as ever, but she still doesn't give me a chance. Ivan's giving her rides in the helicopter almost every day. I wonder if they're landing somewhere and getting it on. But why bother doing that when you can do it in a comfortable sleeping bag. Besides, Ivan doesn't seem interested in her at all. I swear he's in love with that Jet Ranger, the way he takes care of it.

The other day a hundred-hour checkup came up, and do you think he would fly one more minute? Not a chance. For two days the crew had to walk or stay in camp because he was giving his machine the once-over. Getting me to call Mayo for this or that. Well, it won't be long now and this summer will be winding up, I can go back to civilization and girls, girls, girls. The first night I'm out I'm going to find a strawberry blonde with long, long legs. Who needs a lousy bush cook anyway? Look out!

Franklin

The apple of her being in the color of her aura.

I'm still trying to get her to listen to me. If she would let me talk to her for half an hour I could convince her. I've written a whole series of poems to her but she never gives me a chance to read them. I know we have something in common, something deep and spiritual, and if I could only persuade her to meditate with me once, she would see it too. She's like a pillar in the middle of the camp. We all shuffle around her, matrixed. But she refuses to listen, she twists between us and stays herself unmarked.

Yet she is inspiring. If I really want to concentrate, it's her image that hovers behind my closed eyes, the outline of her face and bones. J.L. mystery.

Hudson

I'm damn near ready to crack up. Jerome is in a fearful wax, he gets nastier every day. Reminds me of old Rasky in grammar school, used to cane us just to make himself feel better. Of course Jerome blamed me for that prank. I told him straight out that I didn't start it but that I had to go along with it or the fellows would have called me a peach. Even so, he's pretty sore.

And he's abusive as hell. One day the bastard even kicked me. Guess he thought I wasn't walking fast enough. I almost hauled off and punched him then, but that would only make matters worse. He'd probably have me fired.

God, the time drags. We've got only a month or so left but it seems like forever, I don't know if I can last that long. England seems as far away as another lifetime. I'll go home at Christmas this year, Papa will pay the fare.

I'm on my way back from the latrine one night when I see that her Coleman lamp is still on. Without even thinking, I find myself stopping by her door.

"J.L.?"

She opens the zipper. "What is it?"

"Can I talk to you?"

She looks at me for a moment, then stands aside. "Sure. Come in."

Inside I perch awkwardly on the edge of the cot. Compared to ours, her tent is bare and neat. There's hardly room in those Storm Havens for two and we've got boots and dirty socks and shirts scattered everywhere. Milton may believe in God and keeping his body in shape but he doesn't take to tidiness. He's never washed any clothes, he just keeps wearing them. There's a faint smell of spice in here, a smell I sometimes catch when I'm walking, trudging behind Jerome, but of course I never have time to stop and find out what it is, what kind of plant or flower it comes from.

"What's your problem?" she says.

She's sitting on the other end of the cot and I see that she's sewing, stitching at a tiny, scarlet square of cloth. I can't think what it might be, but seeing her like that, head bent and absorbed with the needle in her hand, she takes on another shape, another image.

I only meant to talk to her, maybe she gets lonely too, but instead I find myself blurting out like a fool, "I wish this summer was over."

She doesn't look up from her stitching. "Why?"

"Everything. Jerome." And I can't speak anymore, I'm choking on my own words, I hold my head in my hands and try not to retch.

"Yes," she says softly, "yes, he's a bad one all right. Lucky you only run into a man like that once in a while or a person would be soured on the whole human race."

"What can I do?"

"Stick it out."

"He's killing me. It's bloody awful." I tug at my hair and groan.

"There'll be a point where he'll stop."

"When? When? I don't care, I just want to get away from him and go home."

"Being homesick doesn't help, does it?"

"Aren't you?"

She smiles. "No. This has been a good summer for me. Of course I miss some people very much, but I'll see them again."

She's so calm, so contained and whole that I would like to shake her, make her feel some anger.

But she's talking, the words falling into the restful stillness of her tent. "He can't do anything to you. He can make you work hard, but he can't do much more unless you let him."

And then it hits me, it pierces the fog in my head. Of course she's right. I've let him think that I won't resist. I don't have to do anything, I just have to make him understand that I would resist. Even so, she's right, he can't do much to me except make me miserable, and if it's me being miserable I can do something about it. In a flash I understand. I can see that the summer will end and when I'm gone I'll have won, I'll have outlasted him.

She's still talking, almost in an afterword to herself. "And homesickness is a fickle feeling. You might discover once you're gone that you're homesick for this place."

"Perhaps."

There's a long silence between us, with only her needle snicking in and out of the bright cloth.

"J.L.? Aren't you ever afraid?"

She lays down the patch of cloth and purses her lips. "Why would I be afraid?" Her eyes are green and depthless, unrevealing. She stands up then, dismissing me, tugs open the zipper and looks at the sky. "It's clear. Get yourself a good night's sleep."

And I do, I sleep sprawled on that sagging cot completely dreamless and numb.

J.L.

Ah Deborah, it's started. They're coming to me one by one, pouring their pestilence into my ears, trying to rid themselves of the poison. I can't blame them, the goddess knows they need to tell somebody, but oh, the weight of those words. They suck at me like quicksand but I have to listen. I know that if I repulse them, they may never speak again, they'll have lost their only opportunity to become men.

Poor children. I thought we women carried heavy bundles. Theirs are that much heavier simply because they cannot admit that they're carrying any. And they come to a woman to lay them down, put them at my feet and expect me to sort the faggots, shape the bundle neat and tidy, so that they can carry on with their predestined world.

Men. A paradox, a quandary, whole centuries of snakes and ladders. I wouldn't trade. And yet they've got it all, they've managed so sublimely to capture the better half of the world and put us to work for them. Nerve, they're born with it, they carry with them blind, unhesitating presumption. After all, it has been given.

And only a man would have the nerve to connect himself with God, to name a part of his very anatomy after a place of worship. The forehead of a man is the seat of wisdom, the place of being, the center of thought. How many of them have we seen posed, head ostentatiously propped on a fist. And temple it is, they worship themselves as intently as we poor females have never dared. Worship their own intellectual capacity when it is (if they only stopped to consider the danger) no larger than ours.

And women, we have no temples, they have been razed, the figures of our goddesses defaced, mutilated to resemble men, even Athena destroyed. Where do you worship when your temples are stolen, when your images are broken and erased, when there is only a pressure at the back of your brain to remind you that we once had a place to worship. Now lost, leaderless, no mothers, no sisters, we wander and search for something we can have no memory of.

Dear Deborah, forgive my carping. I know that in the end what matters most is how we survive. But I find myself raging, I find myself waiting angrily for that promised period of peace. I'm beginning to think that unless we take some action ourselves, it may never come. It's time we laid our hands on the workman's mallet and put the tent pegs to the sleeping temples, if ever we are going to get any rest.

I miss you and I hope your songs are going well.

Thompson

It happens before any one of us is half awake. We're in the cooktent planning the day when Jerome starts yelling outside. He glowered all through breakfast but that's not unusual, he always does. Now he's shouting a string of obscenities and the threat in his voice doesn't bode well. Mackenzie bolts out the door, with me on his heels. Hudson is kneeling on the ground lacing up his boots and doing his best to ignore Jerome.

"Hey, what's going on?" says Mackenzie.

"You keep out of this," shouts Jerome. "Well, what about it, you bastard?"

Hudson flushes. "I don't know what you're. . . "

"You know very well what I'm talking about. Don't lie to me, I saw you, I saw you coming out of that little slut's tent at one o'clock in the morning. What do you expect me to think you were doing? Playing cards?"

"Wait a minute," says Mackenzie.

But nothing can stop Jerome. "Maybe everybody can do what they fucking well please here, but not my assistant. And if he's fucking the cook, then the whole damn camp gets to fuck the cook. We won't have any favoritism here."

By now all the men are outside watching, hostile. Behind Jerome the gray rubble of the rockslide forms an ominous backdrop.

"I was just talking to her," says Hudson.

"I'll bet," says Cap jealously.

"You slut," says Jerome viciously. "No wonder you can't work worth a damn in the day, you're too busy humping all night."

Hudson's face is white now and he stands awkwardly, hands clenched at his sides. "Ask her."

"Ask her?" Jerome hoots. "You don't expect me to believe her! I saw you! You were sneaking out of there with one

174

hand holding your pants up."

And then Hudson hits him. He takes one step forward and shoots out that gangly arm and connects with Jerome's teeth in one smooth crunching second. Jerome staggers back in surprise but then his face flames red and he goes for Hudson. Hudson doesn't move, takes the punch, then lets him have it again, in the eye this time. Jerome is furious, flailing his fists wildly, but Hudson is unmoving. He doesn't hit Jerome again but stands solidly through his glancing blows. That makes Jerome even madder and he punches Hudson in the stomach. Hudson staggers back, then regains his balance and lands a piston-like jab on Jerome's nose. He must have learned to fight somewhere.

Until finally Mackenzie says, "Stop it!" and there is no mistaking the authority in his voice.

"He hit me!" yells Jerome. "Let's finish this." His face is already beginning to swell and his nose is bleeding.

"I'd have hit you too," says Mackenzie. "Stop it."

"He can't get away with this. I'll stomp him." And he rushes at Hudson.

Mackenzie grabs him. "Stop it."

"Well then he's fired," Jerome pants.

"Nobody's fired. You just lost your assistant. Man who badgers his assistant doesn't deserve one."

"You bastard, that little shitface can't get away with anything he pleases."

"That's enough, Jerome!" And I have never before heard that cutting edge of sarcasm in Mackenzie's voice. "I did give you credit for brains. It's none of your goddamn business whose tent he was coming out of and what he was doing there."

"He was just talking to me," says J.L. And adds, in a tone that makes the men look down and shuffle their feet, "Besides, I'm not interested in fucking anybody, let alone the whole camp."

Jerome snarls at her. "You're nothing but trouble, you

little bitch. You think you can get away with everything —
well, you just wait, you little whore."

"I said that was enough," yells Mackenzie, and Jerome
is finally silent.

She only stands there and looks at him, but if he had any
sense he'd leave her alone, he'd navigate a circle around her,
because the day he gets too close to her, she's going to be
ready for him.

"Thompson! Take Jerome and go soak his head," barks
Mackenzie. "And if there's one more ruckus, this whole
goddamn camp is going to be working twenty hours a day for
the rest of the summer. The last thing we need is a fight
about who was coming out of whose tent. All of you, get
your stuff together and get out there and don't come back
until you've done a decent day's work."

If Jerome ever thought he could challenge Mackenzie, he
just proved himself wrong. But there's going to be trouble,
I don't expect this will end here.

Hearne

He really surprised me. You don't expect those skinny English types to throw much of a punch. But boy, does he ever lay into Jerome, like he hates him more than anything in the world. What a sight. Jerome's face is going to look like a purple pin cushion.

So he was in J.L.'s tent. We weren't exactly on his side until he started driving at Jerome. It happened so fast I only got a chance to take a couple of pictures. I hope they turn out, I'd love to have some good shots of a fist fight.

And now Hudson's going to work with me. What's the difference, Franklin or Hudson? Franklin's always stopping behind a boulder to chant, or else he's scribbling in his notebook. I swear his field notes have more poetry than descriptions of rocks. Hudson can't be any worse. Besides, he'll be a different subject to take photos of. Quite a change from Franklin, a scruffy-looking guy who's always philosophizing about life, to a clean-shaven English type who hardly says a word. Where the hell does he get the energy to shave every day?

Milton

They start beating each other, using words I never heard before. It has something to do with the cook, I can understand that much, but why are they fighting when they're both after the same thing in the end.

She holds enough anger inside her to burn a person right through. When Mackenzie stops them, Hudson is over it quick and Jerome is still crazy mad. But she's the one with the anger, she's the one who is full to the brim boiling with fierce pride. Wherever girls are they do that, they start men off so they get thick and angry and full of that dreadful itch. She makes me feel it, even if I know she's not the right kind of girl, she wouldn't be a good woman to have. She doesn't sing while she works, she whistles, she is defiant, she thinks she's as good as any man. When girls get like that, they're no good to marry.

Jerome

This is the last goddamn straw. As soon as I can arrange it, I'm going out for my week off, and I'm going to ask some questions at the office. When the party chief allows all kinds of practical jokes, when the crew can drink and smoke dope until their brains are shit, you don't have a project, you've got a funny farm. What can I say. I've got to blow the whistle on Mackenzie. He's completely fucked up. No wonder this project is a bust, he hasn't concentrated on the property at all, left that to me. He's wandering around to the west of here. Latest thing is, he claims he's found a hot showing, maybe gold. I've seen the samples and they look like pyrite to me. Fool's gold for a fool.

And that bastard Hudson punching me. I guess he got as good as he gave. I wasn't going to stand there and let him hammer at me without hammering back. The guy is mentally unbalanced, can't follow orders, won't work worth a damn, grumbles all the time. Daring to hit me because I tell him that if he's going to screw the cook he's got to share the goods with the rest of the crew. To top it all off, Mackenzie sticks up for him. Oh, I know why. He's protecting the cook. I've seen the way he looks at her. Still, I never expected a forty-year-old man to develop a teenage crush on a bitch like her. She's totally unscrupulous, flaunts herself all over the place, then squeals and says "Don't touch me!" if you come near her. Dumb broad. Thinks that the rules don't apply to her, that she can play both ends against the middle and get away with it. Well, she's going to find out. I'm still waiting for one of the men to pick her up and throw her on the ground, choke her until she gives up and lies still. I'm waiting. And when it happens, I'm not going to lift a finger, I'll be applauding all the way. It's only what she deserves. Let a woman like that get away with being a blue-ball tease and

179

you've done the world a disservice. She'll try to get away with it all her life.

She needs to be taken apart a few times. It's the only thing you can do with a slut like that. Leads those guys on like sheep, cracks some joke and sits there slyly waiting for them to laugh. I know she started that little scenario with the crew acting drunk in the morning. She thought of it and talked them into it and set me up as the fall guy. She thinks she can get away with it. We'll see if she's still in one piece when I get back, the crew's getting pretty restless.

I wouldn't go out if I didn't think I had to rescue this program. Mackenzie tells me that he's not taking a week off this summer, but that won't make any difference to me. I'm going to do my best to get this camp straightened out.

Hudson

I surprised myself. When he starts winging into me I can hardly believe it. The jerk actually thinks he has the right to tell me what I can or can't do. He saw me coming out of J.L.'s tent and of course his mind has only got room for one idea. So he starts having a public fit about it. It's not so much what he says as the way he says it; I've never heard such a foul-mouthed scene.

I try to stay calm, control myself, there's no point getting into a row about it. I'll only get fired if I punch him. But there's something so crude in the look on his face when he says that I was sneaking out of her tent, I don't even know what I'm doing, I just smash my fist at him and smash it again, feel the crunch of teeth and bone under my knuckles without actually registering anything except a red flood in front of my eyes.

It's been a good while since I hit a chap. That was years ago and he beat me, mopped up the playing field with me. I was as mad as he was, but he was twice as heavy as me and I didn't stand a chance. I managed to give him a swollen face and closed one of his eyes, that was all. For a week I could hardly limp around.

When Mackenzie grabs Jerome I stop, stand there waiting for him to flail me up and down for hitting a superior. Instead he rails at Jerome some, then sends him off with Thompson to get cleaned up. I feel my face, discover with some surprise that he's hardly even touched me, the guy can't fight worth pansies. Mackenzie is shaking my shoulder.

"You all right?" he says.

"Yes, sir."

"Don't sir me," he says, "and don't fight anymore. God knows Jerome has a bad temper but it's not worth fighting about."

J.L. says something behind me.

"I know," he says impatiently, "but it doesn't matter. It's none of his business. You," he says to me, "stay away from him. You work with Hearne. I'll send Franklin with Jerome."

I nod, dazed. I don't even have to work with the creep anymore. I turn back to the tent to pick up my pack and see the whole crew standing there, watching. I'm embarrassed, I don't know where to look, but very quietly they shake my hand and thump me on the back and I realize they've all wanted to hit him one time or another this summer, and now I've done it for them.

Mackenzie

M-79-308: Sample description

Mineralized quartz veins.

Visible arsenopyrite cubes with fine-grained disseminated pyrite and arsenopyrite.

Fresh surface gray weathers to brown.

Wall rock extensively altered.

Evidence of widespread hydrothermal alteration — sericitization, silicification and weak to heavy pyrite and arsenopyrite impregnation.

** Note: Reminiscent of Nevada gold deposits.

Ivan

I can tell she's upset. Those guys got it out of their system fighting, but that didn't help her. She's anxious. Guess I would be too if Jerome was after my hide. It's a hard thing for her. She's damned if she do and damned if she don't. So she just goes on cooking like mad. Listens, but never says much.

The day after the fight I have to move Mackenzie and Thompson. I ask her to come along, figure it will take her mind off things. She won't even put on the headphones to talk to me, just sits there and watches the mountains unrolling, watching the valleys feathering down to silver creeks. Broods.

I nudge her, try to cheer her up, but she just shakes her head. Finally I knock her hat off and shove the headphones over her ears. I hate to see her miserable.

"Hey, what's the matter?"

"I just cause trouble," she says.

"Why?"

"It's my fault, isn't it?"

"Because Jerome is a prick and Hudson let him know about it? That was coming a long time."

"But still, it wouldn't have happened without me as an excuse."

"If you hadn't been there, he would have had another excuse."

"Do you think so?" she says doubtfully.

"Listen, this has been a good camp and you've helped. So Jerome gets carried away, some guys get a little horny. That's normal. Happens all the time."

"But he wasn't doing anything except talking!"

"I believe you! Anyway, it doesn't matter."

She grins then. "Well, I'm a good cook."

"Come on, forget it."

When we pick up Thompson and Mackenzie, they're as excited as two magpies. "Hey, look what we found!" They pass J.L. a chunk of rock.

"What is it?"

"Quartz loaded with gold."

"Where?" says J.L. doubtfully.

"It's fine-grained, hard to see with the naked eye. But it's there!"

"Are you sure?"

Mackenzie laughs. "We're getting surer all the time. Wait until the assays come back on this."

We move them further up the valley and then we set out for home. She's still grinning, their excitement has rubbed off on her.

"Well, Ivan," she says, settling back in the seat, "I like to fly."

And I remember Thompson telling me the same thing, asking me to persuade her to actually take lessons. We buzz along for a few minutes. "Did you ever think about learning to fly?"

She eyes me. "You've been talking to Thompson."

I look straight ahead and deny it. "No. You like it. No reason why you can't do something you like for a living."

"Do you honestly think I could?"

"Why not?"

"Money."

"Sure, it costs money. You can get a loan. I did."

She thinks for a moment and then she laughs out loud. "Imagine. If I'm having trouble as a cook, I'd probably have ten times as much trouble as a helicopter pilot."

"I don't know. People have some respect if you can handle a complicated machine like this."

She laughs again. "Sure. But tell me, Ivan, there must be drawbacks even to having magic wings like this."

I nod. "Yup. You can't get careless. You don't go one hour over fifty hours before you check your machine out, and you double-check it at a hundred. It's better if you're your own engineer."

She's looking at me, I can feel her eyes probing my face. "Aren't you ever afraid?"

I watch the altimeter. "I don't think about it."

"But you are."

I nod stiffly, resentful that she's asked the question but only able to tell her the truth.

"Of what?" she asks.

I've never said anything about it to anybody before, I've only sometimes seen it in the corner of my eye, creeping up. I know it's a bad thing, fear. It can make you panic, lose your head, lose control. Pilot error, they call it.

I don't want to answer her. After trying to talk her into lessons, it sounds like backtracking.

"What are you afraid of?" she says again.

I've always thought she was good luck, that if she was in the Jet Ranger with me, nothing could happen. Even so, I don't like talking about this while we're flying, it makes me nervous, it's asking for it, calling disaster down on your head.

But she insists, she asks again, relentless, until finally I can't help myself, I say to her what I've never dared to say to myself.

"Of crashing. Of crashing the helicopter and dying. Of smashing the machine and having the blades cut through the cabin and slice you in half. Of burning up inside the chopper, not being able to get out. Of having some fool walk into the tail rotor and lose his head. And knowing, knowing every day that it will happen because of your mistake, because of the one mistake you're certain to make one day."

The words shock even me, I've gone blind, that crashing behind my skull, only my hand on the stick reminds me that this is really happening. "Yes, goddamn it, I'm afraid. I'm afraid of dying, same as everybody else. And my chances are better than anybody's. But if that was all I ever thought of, I'd never fly and I'd miss half the joy of life."

It's then I feel her hand laid cool over mine on the stick. For a moment everything blurs before I can see again. We're still flying toward camp, the machine around us a steady growl.

"Ivan," she says softly and her voice over the headphones comes from another country, "you won't get killed flying. You'll die in bed. I promise."

And I believe her. Maybe it's irrational, but I believe her.

Roy

Next trip I make what do I get as cargo but Jerome. Guess he's going out for a holiday. I arrive in the morning and the whole crew is in, must be having a camp day. More like a holiday because Jerome's leaving. He's itching to get going so I take my time unloading the food and fuel, and by then it's noon and I don't mind when they ask me to stay for lunch.

Boy, some strange camp. That crew working and clambering over and ignoring the rockslide that practically wiped them all out. They're cheerful as hell. I can't figure whether it's because Jerome is leaving for a week or whether they're just happy. And whatever else that girl does, she can cook. I can't exactly tell what we had for lunch, but it tasted great. Even bakes her own bread. Those men just eat and take her for granted.

When I tell her she's a good cook, Thompson laughs out loud.

"Of course J.L. is a good cook," he says. "What did you expect? She gets her recipes from the bears."

J.L. shakes the soup ladle at him, but you can tell she likes the crew.

After lunch they all sit around reading their mail. I notice Mackenzie got a thick packet of assay results but he doesn't look at them right away. Most geologists tear them open as fast as they arrive. When I ask him whether they're any good, he shrugs. "I'll get to them soon enough." They couldn't have found much here.

"Isn't anybody else going out this summer?" I ask.

Mackenzie shakes his head, grinning. "Nope, we like it up here too much."

So Jerome and me take off back to Mayo and I'll be damned if he doesn't carry on and complain all the way there. Tears apart the camp and the crew and Mackenzie and Thompson and the program, and when he's through you'd swear he'd been working in Siberia with a bunch of criminals. Not to mention what he says about J.L. I have never seen a man hate a woman so bad. I wonder if it has something to do with that shiner he's sporting, but I don't think it would be smart to ask him.

But one thing is sure. When you hear a guy like that carrying on, you know it isn't half as bad as he makes it. By the time we get to Mayo, I'm figuring that it must be a pretty good camp. I'll bet they're delighted as hell that he's gone.

Mackenzie walked down to the lake with us and shook hands and said, "Have a good week, Jerome." The bastard just growled and mumbled something under his breath. Real civil. Lucky me. Next week I get to take him back out there.

J.L.

I can hardly believe the difference it makes when he's not around. I didn't realize how much I watched him, how I never dared to turn my back, how I was always anticipating the moment when he'd try to corner me alone. I can relax for a week. All I have to do is feed these men and keep them happy, wash dishes and burn garbage and haul water and peel vegetables and cook. I don't have to balance myself, always ready, always intuiting his next move.

Men never know what that's like, they never experience the constant awareness that one is vulnerable, open to attack; at any given moment someone who is larger and stronger and angrier can impose himself on you. The only variation is time: when?

It happens to all of us sooner or later. After all, they have the perfect excuse. We get the blame for it. We were in the wrong place at the wrong time, we were dressed the wrong way, we called attention to ourselves. And Deborah, you've had it happen to you so much, simply because you're beautiful. As if we had a choice when the looks were handed out. We're never satisfied. I would still choose to look like you, and you say you would still choose to look like me. Perhaps that's why they call us Siamese friends. The one is wearing the other's costume, we are forever and irrevocably intertwined.

Well, I expect Jerome to rectify his error when he gets back. He'll have to try something before the end of the summer. And Hudson has already shown him that *he* won't take any more nonsense. I only wish I could drive him in the face like that. The feel of bone under your knuckles must be totally satisfying.

I know, we're supposed to change them with non-violence, we're supposed to show them by example, turn an oblique cheek until they wear themselves out. That's the slow way. I can think of a few methods to bring a quicker peace. All we need is the daring, the nerve. Of course, we'll be condemned for acting, we'll be forever traitors and bitches, have broken all the rules of hospitality, but we'll have gotten what we want. Peace. To hell with the historians and analysts. They always decide against us anyway.

Oh, I know all about the exceptions. This camp is full of them. Nice, well-meaning men. They wouldn't deliberately hurt anyone. Yet they've been marinated in it, they've soaked up centuries of divine right. This summer has made me realize a few things. That it's better not to make love to them. When I think of how much I've given out to all the men I went to bed with and how little I got back, I know it's better not to.

If only the real exceptions were easier to discover. Like Mackenzie. He's the only one struggling here and he's the least likely. I've seen him laying himself open all summer, fighting toward a knowledge that he doesn't understand, probably won't understand even when he gets there, and yet he fights for it, against all instinct and against all odds. Even knowing it will be painful, even knowing it might destroy what his life has been up until now.

I respect him. I could love a man like that, maybe relax enough to let him love me. That's the hardest of all. Trusting them.

Send me the words to your new song. I can hum it under my breath while I'm peeling carrots.

Cap

I'm sitting in the cooktent making a list of the soil samples I've just packed to send off, when she comes in and sits down at the end of the table, where she always sits.

"Cap," she says, "I want to take a shower. Would you pour the water in for me?"

"Sure," I say. "Is it heated?" She always asks Ivan to pour her water, like she doesn't trust me or something, but Ivan's gone to pick up Thompson. She's less bristly lately. Maybe she's decided she likes me.

The shower is a great invention but it takes some doing. It's just a wooden frame stall with a tarp tacked around it and an inverted oil drum with holes punched in the bottom on top. If you want a shower you need another person to pour the hot water into the drum and to mix in cold water until you get the right temperature.

I haul some cold water from the lake and mix it with the hot until it's just right, then I pour it into the drum. All the while I can sense her standing naked and shivering inside that tarp-covered shower stall, her head tilted back and the water running down over her shoulders and back and bum. I stand outside the shower and listen. I can hear the liquid movements of her body, she's turning slowly under the water's fall, turning and holding herself up to its warmth. On the ground beside the shower, her clothes lie in a heap. I pick up her T-shirt, rub it against my face, smell cooking and washing dishes and burning garbage and her sweat, and under it all a faint, faint wisp of her own smell, lemony and distant. And before I can think, I'm taking off my clothes, leaving them in a heap beside hers. Hell, if Hudson's coming out of her tent at one o'clock in the morning, why can't I join her in the shower?

I pull aside the tarp and from under the rain of water she looks at me. "It's cold," she says. "Come in."

Her body is pale and fragile, almost a child's, and yet the length of her back, her legs, her nipples erect to the water are so much more beautiful than I imagined, I can hardly breathe. I feel like a stupid lump standing here, so thick and graceless. She turns herself toward me and smiles, then she opens her arms. I stumble into them, clench her against me, feel warm skin like liquid pearls. The water trickles over us, her face is cradled against my chest and her hands caress my back, moving softly. For a moment only the silken feel of her body hammers in my temple and then I lay my head on hers and I cry. My tears mix with the water and I can only stand and hold her and let them fall into her damp, spiky hair. She holds me and comforts me like I'm some big god-damn baby. When the water runs out, she gently steps back and starts to dry herself. She rubs me dry too, without saying a word, just rubs me with the towel, while I wipe at my face with my fist. Then she steps out of the shower onto the moss and there, in the sunshine, she pulls on her T-shirt and her jeans, laces up her shoes and settles her hat on her head, and turns once more to smile at me fumbling into my shorts.

I can't look at her. After all that, walking into her shower and then just holding her and crying, not even remembering sex, not even getting a hard-on. Bawling like some baby.

And then she does the funniest thing. I'm bent over, ashamed, picking up my pants, and she lays her hand on my head, like a blessing. I remember the priest doing that when I was little. She just rests her hand on my head and says nothing, looks at me so warm and gentle I'm suddenly calm, washed clean, complete. That's all. She turns and walks away, and the next thing I remember she's cutting up tomatoes and laughing and joking with Milton and Hearne.

And she doesn't ever say a word, but sometimes she smiles at me and I get that washed-over feeling again. I know if I want to, I can go and hold her and she'll let me, she'll rub my back with that circular motion and murmur softly, but I'll never make love to her. It's like that. Hard to believe.

Thompson

The assay results are unbelievable. Up to three ounces of gold per ton. Of course, it's sporadic and in the wall rocks the concentration is lower, but the quartz veins show up to five ounces a ton.

Unbelievable. When Mackenzie looks at the results he keeps a straight face, just nods and hands them over to me. I can see why he held off, waited to open them until Jerome was gone. Nothing would have made Jerome madder, he's convinced we found some pyrite. I have to laugh out loud. I can hardly believe it. We've found ourselves a goldmine, clear and simple.

Now we've got work to do. We've got to get that area staked up fast and quiet, or we'll have a whole herd of airplanes coming in here. The last thing we want is a staking rush. The crew has some posts cut already, but not nearly enough. We'll stake as many claims as we can. In the Yukon the rules are you can only stake eight claims per person, so we'll have to get everybody out there.

Wait until Katie hears about this. I don't dare to write her now just in case somebody gets hold of the letter, but wait until I tell her. This is the most exciting summer I've had, it's the first time I've ever found anything good. Actually, Mackenzie was the one who found it, who figured there might be gold there. But he's generous as hell, gives me half the credit without even thinking. Really, I didn't do anything. I was just tagging along with him.

Can you believe it? A goldmine because of a useless uranium property. Talk about turning dross to gold. I'm sure it has something to do with J.L. She's brought us good luck.

Mackenzie

Evaluation of showing:

1. Evaluate area for staking.

2. Describe structure and stratigraphy of area.

3. On the basis of evaluation, stake claims (high priority/ low priority).

4. Keep it quiet.

Thompson

We're flying out to the showing to make an evaluation and see how much ground we should stake when Mackenzie suddenly points down a valley we haven't explored at all. "Can you drop us there?"

"Sure." Ivan starts hovering in.

"Hey, that's not our showing," I say.

"I know." Mackenzie grins back at me.

Ivan has trouble finding a clear spot to land down here below treeline. But he finds a bare spot about the size of a dime and manages to squeeze the chopper down. I've never seen anyone with so much nerve.

"Back here in two hours," Mackenzie says to Ivan as he climbs out.

And then we are alone, the swirl of wind and noise receding with the machine. It is so still here, thick and hot, not at all the Yukon I am used to. It's surprising what a change a few miles down the valley can make. There are trees here, a rustling growth that is absent on the mountain, that landscape so stony bare you come to think it alone exists. Even if you can see trees far down the valleys, you don't believe they're real, not until you are among them again.

Like here. A steady whine, and then a sting. "Hey, Mackenzie, there's mosquitoes. What are we doing down here?"

"Exploring."

"Like hell. Getting bitten."

"Come on," he says, "I want to show you something."

Just like him to have worked all the way down here. I follow him through the bush, dodging branches and swearing at the bugs.

After we have walked about half a mile he stops, lifts his hand. "Hear it?"

"What?"

"Listen."

I hear nothing but the rustle of trees.

"Come on," he says.

But after another hundred yards I do hear it, a long, far-away roar that grows larger as we walk, louder and stronger until it overtakes and conceals the sounds of the forest.

And then, without warning, we are standing at the edge of a narrow gorge that is creased hundreds of feet deep into the rock. Over it roars a mountain stream that, in its fall, unleashes itself to brilliant life.

Mackenzie turns to me and grins. "How about that?"

I shake my head and dare to move closer to the edge. "How did you find it?"

He shrugs. "Just walking along one day. Almost fell down there."

I laugh. A cool mist from the water's spray grazes my face.

"Beautiful, isn't it?" he says. "I thought you'd like to see it. Good luck for our showing."

He's never said anything like this to me in all the years we've worked together and I'm speechless, almost overcome.

He laughs again. "Hey, let's see if we can roll that rock over the edge. It'll make a grand splash."

And although the boulder is wedged tightly, we manage to dislodge it, lever it toward the gorge and into the falls. It plummets with a heavy ponderous grace in a final moment of light and color before it smashes to rest against the rocks below.

"Hey," I say. "There's another one."

And again we edge it loose, send it spinning over the side of the beckoning falls to crash through rainbowed water and land with a force that seems to send spray back up to us.

And suddenly we are wild, madmen, rolling boulders down in some aberrant bowling game that scores nothing but mist and spray and dull thunder, that cannot tear the sheet of water the gash in the rock holds in front of itself.

Boulder after boulder we send plunging down the abyss, into the open maw of that lovely chasm. Until finally, exhausted, we are done, the last crash of rock has died and the water continues its remembered and even boom.

Wet and sweat-streaked, we collapse on the ground to catch our breath, together there in an unbreakable joining that transcends us both.

Finally Mackenzie sighs. "Better get back," he says. "Ivan will be slashing trees with his tail rotor."

He sits for a moment longer, then pushes himself up and is walking away when he turns.

"Wait," he says, "J.L."

I stop, wait.

He goes back to the falls and looks down for an instant, then starts walking back up the valley.

"At least," he says to no one in particular, "she'll know we thought of her."

Milton

Every day now we go farther down the valley chopping trees and cutting posts. Even Cap is out here cutting posts. I didn't think I would be doing this, swinging an axe.

They must have found something. They won't say what it is, but they talk about staking in two days and we're working like mad. At night I'm almost too tired to eat, it's sometimes nine o'clock before we get back to camp. When I go to bed, Mackenzie and Thompson and Hearne and Franklin are poring over those maps and when I get up they're still there, like they've never slept. Mackenzie draws diagrams, roughs out a claim location map. He says he needs one more day to check the area before we stake.

Even if we work like dogs, everyone is cheerful. Jerome is gone, nobody talks about him. J.L. makes more coffee, keeps the supper warm. While she waits she sews together puny squares of red cloth. Can't tell what she's making, she isn't the kind who knows how to quilt. I'm waiting for a chance to ask her how you kiss a girl. She could tell me.

Mackenzie

I need one last day to evaluate the area before we stake. We've got to get it done, the longer we wait, the more nervous I get. If we lose this, I'll never forgive myself. It's better than Meteor Ridge by far.

Thompson and I will go out there and double-check to make sure our staking locations are correct. We've got to get all of the main showing covered. It's going to be a long day, so I ask J.L. to pack me a big lunch. She's been so patient the last few days, keeping supper warm until all hours, packing lunches and thermoses of coffee. She's as excited about this as we are.

And then I realize she's never been out on traverse. I bet she'd like to see the showing. She'll probably have to stake some claims, we don't have enough stakers otherwise, it's only fair to show her what we've found. Besides, she needs a day off. The crew will be in camp getting everything ready for the staking. They can take care of themselves for one day.

"Hey, J.L.?"

She's making sandwiches. "What?"

"You want to come out on traverse with me tomorrow?"

She grins, but then hesitates. "I don't know if I can keep up to your long legs."

"We'll use the helicopter all day. This is just one last check. If you get tired, Ivan can buzz you back here."

"Sure. As long as I'm not in the way."

"Don't you want to see the showing?"

"Yeah, okay." And then she cracks a big smile, so I know she's pleased.

I make sure she's dressed warm and she's got a rainsuit with her before we head out the next morning, Ivan and Thompson and J.L. and me. Thompson checks the east side and I check the west. Ivan drops me and J.L. off and then roars away with Thompson.

She trudges along behind me, game as can be, head bent under the hood of the yellow rainsuit. When I split open a fresh quartz seam and show her the visible gold, she gets all excited.

"Didn't you believe us?" I laugh.

"It's different when you see it," she says defensively. "It's realer somehow."

"It's real all right. This is the best thing the company's found in years."

"But you found it."

"What I find belongs to the company. That's why they pay me."

She's turning that chunk of rock this way and that in her hand. "You can see why the alchemists tried to turn scrap metal into gold," she says dreamily. "It looks so effortless hidden in the rock like this. You know, there's a story about an old man who drank a phial of liquid gold and gained eternal youth."

I laugh. "That's what I should do."

She looks up at me from under the dripping edge of her rain hood. "Why?"

"Well, this will probably be my last find."

"You're not going to quit?"

"I'm getting old. Too old to be out in the field anymore. And it's good to go out with a bang. If this turns into a mine, I'll be fixed."

She's still turning the rock, as if seeing something in its face. "What will you do?"

"Seek my fortune. Something different, I guess. Become an expert."

She only looks at me, penetrates my own questions with her eyes.

But Ivan comes back to move us and I'm checking another location before I dare to think of asking her. She's standing close to me looking at another sample I hold in my hand, our hoods bent together against the driving rain, when she puts her head back and looks up full into my face. Once again I find myself caught, transfixed by her eyes pulling at me, pulling me open. And this time I can't break free, I find myself falling into her invitation, the waiting confessor behind those pupils. I have never yet said a word to her about Janice, but I do not have to explain to her at all. She knows.

I hesitate, stumble and grope for words. "Why? What did she want?"

J.L. looks down, rubs her thumb against the grain of the rock. "Don't you know?"

I shake my head, dumb.

"Do you think she left because you treated her badly?"

"No."

"Do you think she left because you treated her well?"

"No."

"How long did it take you to ask why?"

I lower my head, hating to admit. "Ten years."

At that she looks bemused. "You know," she says, "this rock isn't any good unless you know what it is. It wasn't gold until you discovered it, it wasn't even here until you found it." She turns and heaves the sample away. It clinks down the mountain slope. Then she faces me again and takes my sleeve. "She left for herself. You were a good man but you couldn't give that to her, it had nothing to do with you. It was herself she was after and the only way she could find that was by leaving."

"But," I stumble, "I wouldn't have prevented her from doing what she wanted."

"That's it right there. The very idea that you could allow her or prevent her. That's why she left."

I'm stunned, shocked into silence, and then feel I have to defend myself. "Can you believe that I didn't mean to?"

"Of course," she says. "All that socialization, all that pressure. Not your fault. But then, don't blame her for taking the drastic way out."

It is the sound of my own assumption that hammers in my temple. I grip the handle of my hammer, try to drive away the hubris I have committed, believing that another life could be at my disposal, that I had any right to try and make it so. The dizzy blackness I feel is shame, nothing more or less than shame.

And then it clears, the curtain of rain still falls cool on my face. I'm standing high on a mountain beside a small woman who is holding one of my hands in both of hers.

"After all," she says, her fingers around mine warm and reassuring, "you've redeemed yourself by arriving at that disagreeable knowledge. Most men don't want to know and even if they do, they won't accept the truth."

The irises of her eyes could widen indefinitely to enclose me. If I could become a figure inside those bottomless pupils I would be saved, redeemed. But she'll go too when the summer is over, she'll vanish into a world of her own making, and we men will be left with only the smell, the taste of her.

She reaches up a hand then and brushes rain from my face. "Not yet," she says softly. "Not yet. Don't get ahead of yourself. Remember when that happened last? I had to tell you I was a girl!"

I laugh. "You must have thought I was totally obtuse."

She shakes her head. "Only unprepared. At least you'll never make an assumption like that again."

"I'll never make any assumptions again." And far away, between the hiss of the rain, I hear the thump of the helicopter as Ivan levels it over the valley to top the ridge. We wave and he needles the machine down into the wind. Crouched against the rain and the singing blades, we race for the chopper. And pulling open the door to climb in, she flings back her hood and grins at me over her shoulder.

"Come on, King Midas," she says, "we better stake these claims."

Hudson

This is more exciting than I ever thought. We're staking, we've actually found something! The helicopter drops us off on the mountain with a bundle of posts and we have to stake, we have to hammer the posts into the ground and heap stones around them. Jerome isn't even around to spoil the fun, to scoff and mock and make everybody miserable. This is the way I expected geology to be in Canada. It's damn hard work but it's real, you can find stuff here.

Incredible. A gold deposit. Wait until I tell this story at home!

Ivan

The whole camp is in a frenzy. Somebody thought they heard an airplane this morning and they're all beside themselves. They're going to get that area staked in three days if it kills them. Mackenzie gives orders and I drop them off at an approximate spot with their bundle of posts and they're running, literally running up and down the mountains putting in those posts. Nothing like a staking rush to get everybody going. Especially a gold rush.

It's strictly illegal to drop stakes from the helicopter and Mackenzie does everything straight by the book, so those guys are really working. They're walking and climbing harder than they have all summer. And excited! They're like little kids. Franklin sits in the back of the helicopter and sings at the top of his lungs. Hearne has festooned himself with orange flagging — he looks like a crosswalk. Even Milton tries to outdo himself by carrying more posts than anyone else. And Hudson, well; he's lost his British cool completely.

I'm so busy running everybody around, I can hardly keep track of them all, so I just listen to Mackenzie. He's got everything under control. The Midas claims, he calls them. Wearing a grin so wide I swear it'll crack his face.

And J.L. Gives me a wink once in a while. Keeps that cooktent warm, keeps the coffee on the stove. Feeds them when they come in and feeds them before they go out. Watches and laughs and hands around the scotch bottle.

By God, a person hardly has a chance to piss, but this is the most fun I've had in years.

Mackenzie

Staking:

1. Cut posts.

2. Post location — line cutting.

3. Stake — put posts in ground (2-post system).

4. Send claim affidavits to mining recorder for recording.

5. When tags are issued, tag posts.

Thompson

The Midas claims. I love the sound, it's the perfect name for this discovery. Franklin says it's bad luck, that King Midas wasn't a happy man, but Mackenzie says J.L. gave him the idea and I'm with her for luck any day.

We've been working like crazy for two days and tomorrow we should finish off. Mackenzie wants to make sure we haven't missed any potentially good areas; it's embarrassing if somebody stakes next to you and gets the best stuff. Mackenzie is happy as hell, he's completely forgotten whatever was bugging him before. The whole crew is happy. Nothing like a little excitement to make people work well together.

It's a two-post system in the Yukon. One initial post and one final post to indicate the end of the claim, 1,500 feet long. The only drawback is, one person can only stake eight claims up here. We've already staked eight for everybody in the crew, so if Mackenzie wants to stake some more tomorrow, we'll have to use J.L. That'll mean eighty claims in the grouping. If we haven't covered the deposit with that, I don't know.

What a feeling. It's strange, in the day-to-day slogging of geology you forget the thrill of finding something really good, of knowing that you've discovered what could become a mine. It's every geologist's dream.

The next morning Mackenzie says, "J.L.? You mind giving us a hand today?"

Her face lights up. "Do I get to stake?"

"Yes. We need you to cover a section that I don't want to leave open."

She's ready to go before the men have finished breakfast, as if this is the greatest event of the summer. I can't blame her. Staking, actually finding something and marking it.

We fly out in the chopper with Franklin and Hearne. We'll carry her posts after we get dropped off and I'll tell her where to put them, but she'll get to put them in the ground.

And she does it, she stakes eight claims. Pounds the post into the ground and heaps rocks around it so it won't fall over. Inscribes the post with the claim name and number, the time and date, direction to the number two post, distance to the right or left, and her own name, J.L. At the end of the day she's so tired she can hardly walk but she's completely satisfied with herself.

She is hammering the last post when from the corner of my eye I see a distant movement along the flank of the mountain. Franklin stands a few yards away and Hearne is — what else — taking a picture, but J.L. and I both see the shape, the shadow that crosses a last patch of waning light. We are instantly alert, honed in its direction, its infallible pull. Slowly, with infinite leisure, the shadow lumbers across the mountain's long reach, moves up a small cirque to the ridge.

J.L. inscribes the post, heaps stones around the base, all the while straining toward the shadow. It moves indolently across the cirque, stops to sniff and grub. Hearne has taken his picture and Franklin turns to say, "Chopper's coming."

J.L. throws one desperate look at me, but already the sound of the rotor is growing closer, heavier. I can see her eyes scanning the ridge, in an effort to discover the shape in the ripening dusk, but it seems to have vanished, there is no movement at all.

The helicopter settles itself beside us, and Franklin and Hearne are already in. "Wait," she says. "Please wait."

And I too search the ridge for movement. Acknowledgment. But it is dead, empty.

Her eyes fly once more and below the whine of the blades I hear a low cry of despair before she turns and climbs into the front seat of the chopper.

I sit behind her, put my hand on her shoulder, but she wants no comfort from me. She wants the bear.

The helicopter lifts and turns and then just as we dip along the angle of the ridge, the bear rises, monstrous, unforgiving, filling the frame of the sky between the mountain slopes, her silhouette like a huge, ragged omen against the light. Her claws rake the air — closer, and she would tear us out of the sky, pull us down to her bountiful embrace. She fills our eyes and then, just as quickly, drops to all fours and is gone, once more the ridge between the mountains swept empty.

Hearne and Franklin and Ivan see nothing. But I saw the edges of J.L.'s mouth curve, I saw her lips move in a secret prayer, an invocation.

I am, finally, exhausted.

At the camp everything is silent, no one around. I suspect they've all gone to bed, tired out, but when we push into the cooktent they are all there, shouting and waving. "Surprise!" They have decorated the cooktent with flagging streamers, supper is ready and someone has made a cake with "Midas claims" written in chocolate icing on top. The party is really for J.L. They sit her down and they won't let her do a thing, they stand over her and serve her and ask her if everything is all right. Turns out Milton cooked supper. He didn't do a bad job, even if he can't exactly cook like J.L. She laughs and compliments everything.

We break out a few bottles that night, we build a roaring fire and sit around and drink and tell stories until two o'clock in the morning. There's nothing like staking to make a geologist happy. And when we stumble off to bed, Mackenzie calls after us, "Don't bother getting up tomorrow. We'll take the day off."

I'm going to stay up and write Katie a long letter, try to explain to her what J.L. helped me to understand. This has been such a summer I almost hate for it to end. Still, I'm anxious to get back to her, now things will be even better.

Hearne

I have it. I've taken the perfect photograph. Finally. And I almost missed it, I almost let it slip by me like so many others have, lost possibilities.

We're standing patiently in the waning light, waiting for J.L. to pound her last post. The cast shadow of the mountain reaches long and blue down the valley, the threading off of a day.

J.L. has been so determined, pounding her posts, heaping stones around them so they won't fall, inscribing them with the proper information. She does it all with an intent seriousness that makes me think this staking has another importance to her, this is her farewell ritual to the Yukon, an act of reference for her.

Thompson is steadying the post while she lifts the hammer to pound it into the ground, the slightness of her body straining to hit quick and effective, the tableau of her movement striking a chord so far within me that I almost gasp. This is my perfect picture.

I can hardly fumble my camera from my pack, open the case and remove the lens cap and focus on her standing over that stake, leaning herself and the hammer into the ground until she becomes a movement of striking, driving that post deep into the temple of the earth, driving it smooth and sure and knowing absolutely where it will go. For a moment it is as if she is hammering that stake into everything I have ever known or photographed, hammering the very pulse of life. And then I have it, I have clicked the shutter and caught the perfect picture forever. I close the camera, I know I can take only one. Of the perfect picture there is only one, you would ruin it by taking more.

The post firmly in the ground, she turns and the moment is gone, lost forever. Except for the shadow of her shape that I've kept, the perfect picture will never again exist.

Milton

I saw them. I was running behind the camp, running over the rumpled ground to get away from the drinking and the fire, and I saw them. The rest of the crew stumbles off to bed and only the two of them are left, looking at each other over the fire. Mackenzie doesn't say a word to her. He gets up and he walks, stooped and long-legged, to his tent. She follows him, she walks silent behind him. At his tent door he turns, holds the flap aside for her and then follows her inside. They do not light a lamp, there is no flare of a match. But the zipper is open, forgotten.

I couldn't help myself. I drop to my belly, my hands and knees, I crawl to the side of the tent, stretch myself flat along the ground. No sound, only the distant splash of the lake. I crawl closer, angle myself so I can see through a crack in the open tent flap.

What unfolds for me leaves me rooted to the ground, I could be hammered into the moss. She is standing in front of him in the space between the two cots, and he is unlayering her, taking off her clothes. I hardly know whether to run or to stay, but I'm caught here, hooked. First comes the denim jacket, then a nylon shell, a thick sweater, a shirt, her T-shirt, her jeans, her underpants. Even her shoes and socks, he lifts them off her skin as if he peels an orange. Then she is completely naked, standing in the puddle of her clothes straight and proud. Not an inch of shame to her skin. And her body is alight, it reflects a heat and radiance that I never thought bodies could possess. Luminous glass, perfectly turned.

He bends toward her, does not touch her with his body but flickers his lips over her face, her neck, her arms. She turns this way and that for him, inviting, holding herself there just beyond his hesitating grasp.

He touches her, takes the narrow bone cage of her body

211

and turns it between his hands, carefully, exploring, holds her and smooths her and shapes her between his calloused hands like a forming vase, like a shape becoming.

And then I see him gather her against the roughness of his boots and jeans and flannel shirt, pull her body close to him and see him kiss her.

That is how you do it.

But I expect more, I expect he will do something else to her. He doesn't, he only goes on turning her between his hands, turning her this way and that as if he is discovering in her shape something new for himself. He runs his hands over the outline of her body as if he would memorize her, cherish her in a secret place forever.

And then it's over. She steps into her clothes and she closes herself up and reaches for her hat where it lies on Jerome's cot. They do not see each other and they do not speak. She walks through the door and is gone, her feet sinking springy in the moss on the way to her own tent.

But I saw it, the terror and joy hammered in me. That is how you make a kiss.

Mackenzie

I didn't ask her to follow me. I didn't ask her to come to my tent and open herself up for me, let me gather her between my fingers. It brought me back to Yellowknife, her standing there in that grubby can, looking at my cock and telling me that she's a girl. Only now I know she's a woman and the telling is in the touch.

Let me never again take for granted the wonder of a skin like hers, the flush and pallor of her soft acceptance, the way she turned her body this way and that for me so that I could get a sense of it again, a woman, the way a woman feels.

She turned herself inside my hands, with each movement the porcelain clarity of her skin more luminous, as if my hands could ignite a light within her.

And then she holds me, we hold each other in a great groaning circle of a kiss that wheels and tumbles and transfixes us, that leaves us empty and replete and completely overtaken.

And whatever she did it for, I know that there will never be another to feel like that.

J.L.

If only for him, I've redeemed myself, I've rescued rather than damned. The feel of his rough hands on my skin, turning my body between his palms so gently as to wake me from the longest sleep, a song of praise unlike any other, a promise of hope, an invitation to the perfect years of peace. Tonight I'll rest. They're fed and they're confessed and they're redeemed and I have done nothing more than what I had to do. For that, I'll rest my case.

P.Q.

Jerome comes in full of stories about fights and drinking and random exploration outside of the property. According to him, Mackenzie's program isn't going so well. I'm not worried. I trust Mackenzie and I suspect Jerome is exhibiting symptoms of professional jealousy. Still, this was a big project with a big budget. Maybe it's time Mackenzie thought about giving up fieldwork and settling down in the office.

In the end, I decide to fly back in with Jerome, have a look at the property and the camp now instead of waiting for the supervisors' visit and tour. Besides, I'd like to get out in the field for a week. Be a nice break.

From the air, the camp looks deserted in the early morning sunshine. It seems to balance right on the edge of the lake, as if that massive rockslide shoved it there from further up the valley.

We angle in until the skis dip the water, taxi and then turn and motor up to the camp. It looks abandoned, nobody comes down to the shore, nobody's around.

The pilot steps out on the float and jumps to shore, secures the plane. "Doesn't look like anyone's home," he says.

"See what I mean," says Jerome.

I step out on shore and shout "Hello."

There's no answer. I shout again, at the top of my lungs. "Hello!"

The pilot looks at me and shrugs. If it weren't for the tents, you'd never believe there had ever been anyone here.

"They've probably all developed crotch rot," says Jerome.

There's an imperceptible stirring, a rustle, and then, slowly, creakingly, the camp wakens, the crew begins to emerge one by one, stepping into boots and buttoning shirts, squinting up at the sun. Mackenzie comes around the corner of the cooktent, shrugging into his jacket. He stops in surprise when he sees me.

"P.Q.? What are you doing here?"

"I come to visit you every year."

He looks puzzled. "Is this your yearly tour? Kind of early, aren't you?"

"Well. . . " I try to be diplomatic. Obviously, if they're sleeping in until eleven o'clock in the morning, Jerome has a point; this camp lacks discipline. "I figured I'd come out a little earlier, see how you guys were getting on."

"We're getting on fine. Haven't you seen my monthly reports?"

"Yes, but we heard you had some difficulties here."

"Difficulties? Difficulties?" Then Mackenzie seems to understand, he throws back his head and laughs aloud.

"Well, it hardly gives one an impression of confidence to fly into a camp at eleven in the morning and discover everyone still asleep."

"P.Q." Mackenzie grabs me by the arm and starts to lead me to the cooktent. "I want to show you something. You too, Jerome. Come along."

He is grinning like crazy, and I wonder what's got into him. I've never seen him so high-pitched. In the cooktent he grabs a chair, holds it for me. "Here. Sit down, P.Q." Then he grabs a sample bag, opens it, lays a chunk of quartz-veined rock on the table in front of me. He opens another bag, hands me another sample, and still another.

"Well," he says, "what are you waiting for? Look at them. You want to borrow my hand lens?"

I pick up the first sample, hold it up to the light and instantly catch my breath. I've seen gold before, but this is the first time I've seen a sample like this outside a mine. I pick up the next sample and it's even better, the stuff is as plain as the nose on your face. Mackenzie is leaning against the table grinning at me, and Jerome is looking back and forth from him to me.

"Well, what is it, P.Q.?"

"Looks like there might be some gold here."

"Isn't that interesting?" says Mackenzie. "Now what would you do if you found stuff like that?"

"I'd stake it."

"But we're too busy drinking and carousing and fooling around with the cook and pissing the company's money away. We don't find anything, we just stay up all night and sleep all day!" And he laughs again.

I look at him, shake my head in amazement. I knew I didn't have to worry about him, but I didn't expect a gold-mine.

"Well, P.Q.? What do you say?"

I heft that gold sample in my hand and grin. "I sincerely apologize for giving you shit for sleeping in. And I'd like to see the showing."

"Apology accepted. Let's go get Ivan and head for the Midas claims."

Poor Jerome. It's tough competing with a guy like Mackenzie.

Jerome

It's her fault that I feel so rotten. Without her the whole summer would have been different, none of this stuff would have happened. But get a woman in camp and she makes trouble, she does nothing but stir up shit. Well, I've had it. I, for one, think it's time she got put in her place, taken down a peg or two. The little bitch needs to be taught a lesson and I guess I'm the only one with balls enough to do it.

She set the crew against me, she's sucked in Mackenzie, she's made me look like a fool, and nobody does that to me and gets away with it.

Mackenzie is dead asleep in the other cot. Cautiously I reach under my cot, let my fingers close around the handle of the Magnum, feel its weight against my hand. I slide out of my sleeping bag, lay the gun on the bed while I pull on my pants and slip into my shoes, then pick it up and carry it with me into the night.

J.L.

For a moment he took me by surprise. I wasn't ready for him tonight. I was uneasy all right, waking and sleeping, waking again. So that I couldn't tell, were the footsteps sleeping or awake? And the zipper sliding on my tent, was that a dream? Of course, the instant he jumps on me, the instant I feel his weight smashing onto me, I know. I can hardly wriggle underneath him, but a part of my brain tells me that he can't do anything as long as I'm inside the sleeping bag. And then I feel the barrel of that gun against my head.

"Come on, you little bitch, come on out."

I make myself move, make myself unzip the bag and push my body free, first my arms, then my legs. I know he won't think twice about using that gun, maybe he won't shoot, but all he has to do is knock me on the head. When I'm almost out and half lying on top of the sleeping bag, he fumbles at his pants. In a wild moment of lucidity I almost laugh at his ineptness. He's kneeling over me and he raises himself to get at his zipper just enough for me to bring my knees up and kick full force against his groin. He yells but I don't give him a chance to recover. I knee him again and again, all the while fighting for that Magnum, trying to pry it loose from his raw-boned hands. And then he falls and I've got it, I'm standing over him with a loaded gun.

He tries to get up, lunges for me again, but I wave the gun at him.

"You wouldn't dare," he grunts. "Drop that gun."

"Oh yeah? I'd like nothing better than to blow your balls off."

"Just try it," he says. "You don't have the nerve."

There is a haze of blood behind my eyes and I know now I could fire a gun at him and hit him and never be sorry. I point the gun at him and pull the trigger, but he has been cautious enough to put it on safety. I unclick the safety, point at his crotch.

"Hey," he yells. "Don't be crazy."

I hesitate, then I point the gun up at the tent and fire.

Mackenzie

It's almost as if I wake before the shot, before the gun goes off. The bang is just a confirmation of my knowing that what I was afraid of for so long has happened.

It seems as if I'm up and running toward her tent before I hear the gun go off, as if it's going off again and again and I'm running in slow motion, too late. Finally I get there, it takes forever stumbling over the uneven ground but I get there and tear through the open zipper and stop.

J.L. is standing over Jerome, holding his Magnum in her hand as fierce and steady as an old warrior. But after my first relief that she's all right, the sight chills me. In her long flannel shirt, her bare legs gleaming through the pale twilight of the tent, she seems vulnerable until I hear her voice. I know that voice, she's talked to us all summer, she's laughed and told stories and she's whispered to me. But not in this voice. She's holding that deadly pistol at a point directly between Jerome's legs where he lies writhing on the floor of the tent.

"Just try to get up," she says. "Just try to get up, you bastard, and I'll blow your balls off. That's the only language you understand."

He's trying to crouch himself away from the point of the gun's muzzle, but she follows him mercilessly.

"If you've got any," she says. "I'm probably only shooting at air. So what harm is there? Why don't I try it?" And she clicks back the bolt.

She is sprung there, holding that gun, and suddenly without any doubt at all I know that she would do it, shoot him right between the legs and take the consequences.

"J.L.!"

She holds herself rigid for a moment, then says softly, "Do you think he's got any balls, Mackenzie?"

"Come on, put the gun down. You don't want to do that."

"Oh yes, I do. I'd like to find out." She shifts the muzzle slightly to the left.

"It won't help," I say quietly.

She slumps a little then and I see her letting go, releasing her hold on that furious determination.

"Well, there he is," she says. "He tried to rape me. Not very good at handling a woman and a gun at the same time." She hands me the gun and gestures at Jerome. "Get him out of here."

I haul Jerome out; he's shaking so hard he can't even speak.

When I get back to her she's inside her sleeping bag, curled up into a ball so tight I think she will never unfurl, even when I hold her in my arms and rock her, hold her and tell her over and over and over again, "I'm sorry, I'm sorry."

Deborah

"Most blessed of women be Ja-el,
   the wife of Heber the Kenite,
   of tent-dwelling women most blessed.

He asked water and she gave him milk,
  she brought him curds in a lordly dish.

She put her hand to the tent peg
   and her right hand to the workmen's mallet;
she struck Sisera a blow,
   she crushed his head,
   she shattered and pierced his temple.

He sank, he fell,
   he lay still at her feet;
at her feet he sank, he fell;
   where he sank, there he lay dead."

Here is my song.

Franklin

We found them later, back in town; we found them in our duffel bags and our suitcases and our packsacks. Searching for clean socks, I am surprised when my fingers encounter a patch of something small and soft. So I grab it and pull it out. For a moment I'm not even sure what it is, a small square of scarlet cloth that seems to be a sachet of some sort, and then I realize. The small red square smells the way she smelled, it has that faint lemony scent of the tundra.

So that's what she was doing, gathering moss and sewing it into sachets, capturing the smell of the tundra for us. She went around and left them in our belongings like a token, a pungent memory. The smell of her there, between my dirty socks and underwear, makes me see that in something so small, so pure, there is perfection. And she has given it to us. I press the small, silken square to my nose and inhale that smell, know that I'll never be able to forget either her or this summer.

J.L.

And now the light tumbles, the fire tumbles, the words tumble over and above, falling into the greedy brightness of the flames below. We are burning the summer: old boots and torn bush clothes. The plywood table, on which I thumped bread dough, rolled pie crust, floured chicken and beef, is standing with its two-by-four legs in the ashes. The flames dance beneath it.

I am finished with confession and repentance. I've heard enough of the words that tumble and fall beyond me now, bright as the blood that seeped into the ground. I will not play Joan of Arc and be encindered for what I have been forced to hear, for what I could not escape. Instead, I'll play siren, put on the gypsy skirt that has been collecting creases in the bottom of my knapsack these three months, gather it in my hand and jump atop that sagging table to give them one last word, one final invocation to send them on their way.

The fire beneath me, I can feel its scarlet tongue on my soles, no dancing slippers, only the transformed clump of my thick boots on the buckling plywood. And I lift up my arms and I whirl, the skirt heavy around my thighs, dance for them until that table shivers. Whirl and kick in the ecstasy of the flames beneath me, devouring the summer under my feet.

Above, the stars flare too, in a hiss of sympathy for our bright spark in the pitch landscape. The somber mountain slopes lean over us, even in the darkness ominous, waiting for our retreat.

Around the fire they stand a circle of blurred faces, indistinguishable now as I whirl, sway to the music of the flames. Each one clear to me, the planes and angles of his face as the words tumbled from his lips. Their eyes lift to follow the career of my body, breasts and hips alive with the tingling fire. For a moment I can pretend I am Deborah celebrating myself, victory, peace regained. And in their faces I see my transfiguration, themselves transformed, each one with the tent peg through the temple cherishing the knowledge garnered in sleep, in unwitting trust.

The table beneath my feet begins to slide, to subside into the arms of the fire. At the moment it quivers and crashes I am held for an instant in frozen hiatus and then I leap free to the cool dark edge of the circle.

They can rest now, we can all rest.

Mackenzie

She danced for us, she seemed to appear on that table from nowhere, that table we had pounded our fists and leaned our elbows on and eaten from and played poker at and unrolled maps upon. Naked, the oilcloth gone, the wood already seething in the heat, she leapt upon it and decorated it with the patterns of her bare feet, with the sweep and swish of that impossible skirt.

I want to shout, "You'll fall, you'll burn!" but my throat is thick and numb. She leans down and smiles at me, moving in the pattern of her dance, that marble-smooth body under the cloth arching and circling.

Ah Sisera, I would trade with you. I would give all I had to die at her hand, to have her offer me bread and milk, to feel her smoothing a rug over my tired frame and, yes, to lie asleep and innocent as she lays one hand on the mallet and the other on the tent peg and gently, oh so gently that I might never wake, nails me to the earth, pierces my ear, my temple, with her loving wrath and bestows on me respite, peace.

She celebrates herself, the table disappearing so that it seems she dances over flames, nothing to separate her from the molten heat and light but her steps, her wildly sensual movement to an unheard music, that of tambourines and golden trumpets.

When the table falls, crashes down into the fire, she seems to hang for a moment above the flames, and then one swift movement and she stands beside me, panting, laughing, no longer the witch, the saint of fire, but our own J.L., flat and skinny as before. But her shining face will not let me forget that I have seen her, turned her between my hands. And as I touch her, lay my arm across her shoulder, I know the peg still lodges in my skull. I will never forget.

THE NEW CANADIAN LIBRARY LIST

Asterisks (*) denote titles of New Canadian Library Classics